Life

on the

Grocery Line

A FRONTLINE EXPERIENCE
IN A GLOBAL PANDEMIC

Adam Jonathan Kaat

Inspired Forever Books
Dallas, Texas

Inspired Forever Books™
"Words with Lasting Impact"
Dallas, Texas
(888) 403-2727
https://inspiredforeverbooks.com

Library of Congress Control Number: 2021905692
Paperback ISBN 13: 978-1-948903-77-6
Printed in the United States of America

For Mom and Dad. You picked me.
Thank you for that, and everything else.
I am a lucky man.

And, to all those finally deemed "essential,"
just know you always were, and you always will be.

Table of Contents

February, 1st 2023

The oddly quiet yet personally important three-year anniversary of my start date at "Dream Grocers" passed a couple of days ago. It went by without so much as a whisper until that evening, as I sank into the abyss that is my smartphone, where social media reminded me of both the good and ill of my past.

There it was, plain as day, lambasting me in the blue light of modernity: *"Looks like I'll be ringing you up at your Dream Grocers while I work on my novel instead of that cubicle life. Wooo! Sooo happy to be pushing toward something I dreamt of doing for so long. Come by and say Hi!"*

That Facebook post simultaneously reminded me of how far I've come, what the job meant to me, and how I'm not quite where I want to be yet. I think that's a good thing because that's how time works, right? We are obsessed with it, but it gives zero fucks about our concerns and just keeps moving, on and on.

My neurosis about accomplishments shouldn't matter here because I have this book to remind me of my time in the grocery store. What else am I looking for here? A novel—a volume of my written words on paper and in digital form—is about as permanent a fixture in culture and time and place as one could expect to contribute. It wasn't insignificant. What everyone went through in 2020 and 2021 was no small thing either.

No matter what your thoughts are on the pandemic of 2020, it was culturally, politically, and economically important on a global scale. If you're reading this in the year 2070 and I'm dead or my consciousness has been uploaded to the internet, then you might not see how the world changed in just a couple of years after the time frame of my novel. Or maybe you understand it on a deep level—and I am a fool who is missing the real point. Either way, it mattered, and we shouldn't forget. This isn't a call to dwell on it or inhibit your life in any way, but again, time doesn't stop, right?

Maybe what I am looking for in this prologue and second edition of the book is a self-reminder to be thoughtful and live in the here and now.

At the three-year mark, I left the grocery world, but I realize it hasn't left me. Whenever I go into a supermarket, retail store, or restaurant, I have visions of the dystopian past we experienced. A shiver runs down my spine as I watch someone complain at the customer-service desk over the price of sliced ham or toilet paper. Remember when everyone ran out of shit-tickets? That's why I chose the new cover for this edition. I'll never forget those empty shelves, the hoarding of random items, and the fear in people's eyes.

That same person berating a helpless customer-service worker was probably breaking down in tears at my register only a couple of years ago over the uncertainty they felt. And they would've stabbed another person for getting too close to them in the checkout line. Times change quickly. Humans are both wonderful and cruel in the same breath. I believe that with all my heart, but I wish they were the former more often when talking to those who work in their service.

At this juncture, I have stumbled back into a corporate cubicle life, but this time I feel like I have the upper hand. My dreams are congealing with my reality. Writing is my future. The rest is only noise.

Many things have changed since I wrote *Life on the Grocery Line*—others have not. The remnants of the confusion and overreach are burrowing into the culture like ticks. For all intents and purposes, the pandemic is over except in the hearts of some politicians grasping at straws and trying to wield power over others.

People still wear masks, but there isn't a government mandate. Everything is pretty much back to "normal." Time marches on. The culture wars and doom-scrolling continue at the same rate, and with every new headline, the world is ending in some unforeseen way. The one hope I had for humanity at the beginning of the pandemic was that it might flatten our society and we would emerge with hearts opened to our fellow human beings, especially for those who work in customer service. Maybe it did for some. I don't see the difference when I'm out in the world. Perhaps it's too early to tell. The 2070 reader will have a better perspective.

I'll leave you with a note that is both happy and sad. Life is about balance, I think, but what the hell do I know, really? I'm just stumbling around on this planet, like the rest of us, hoping to find some peace. There is a sadness to the fact I haven't seen most people from Dream Grocers in person since I left the place. And I've reminisced over drinks with a few of them a handful of times. It's not because I don't love them anymore or cherish their amazing energies and stories. It's simply because we have the internet and are still connected through social media. We live busy lives. They are doing big things, and that fills me with joy. I smile when I see their dreams come true and support them when I can. But time is speeding up, and we have only so much of it to spare.

Chapter One

I t's my second day at work; the pace is starting to pick up. From the express lane, I look over the aisles and islands filled with food and patrons. A grocery store is a lightning rod of energy and commotion where the world begins and ends in a spectacularly mundane fashion. Children are running from their mothers and fathers. In every direction people are yelling and complaining and laughing. It's controlled chaos, in a sense, held together by invisible norms forged through evolution and social conditioning. I absorb this curious and lively Institution of Americana with accidental ease, like a toddler learning words, but it's hard to keep up.

I walk toward the registers, my head on a swivel as people come to me with all manner of questions. They see Dream Grocers prominently displayed in bright orange on my black apron like a beacon to all those hopelessly lost and in search of the items they need.

"Where is the European-style braised veal chops with those delicious potatoes? You know the tiny ones?"

I look at the woman for a moment with wide eyes. She stares back, clearly annoyed that I don't know where her item is located.

"I'm sorry. I'm new. Here, let me ask my supervisor Alejandro."

"Don't worry about it. I'll just look around." Before I can ask for direction, she is gone.

Just yesterday, in orientation, Alejandro told me that my first few shifts would be a flurry of information and sound. The clientele at this particular location doesn't have patience, and they will assume I know what they want before they even speak.

A heavy hand falls onto my shoulder; it's Alejandro. "It's not that bad, man. You will get used to it. Just ask one of us if you don't know something," he says with a hearty laugh. Alejandro seems affable and is genuinely helpful. I get the feeling I'm going to enjoy working with him. "Alright, Daniel, we will put you on the express lane for a while until you get used to how the job works. Sound good?"

"Whatever you need, brotha!" I say as I salute him.

He laughs and says, "That's exactly the right idea. Have fun with this, man. It can be a fun job if you take it all in stride."

He sets me up on one of the registers, promises to be right back, and then walks away. I can see him talking to another supervisor. But standing there all alone in a world of which I have only a passive understanding fuels my adrenaline rush over the unknown, and I wait for him to return so I can get to work. He will be shadowing me for the next two shifts, like training wheels for a child learning to ride a bike, and then I will be sent out into the madness of this incredibly busy store to face my own demise.

I look over at the bigger registers, and they seem intimidating. Garbage-dump mountains of groceries speed down twelve lanes of bedlam and are funneled neatly into brown paper bags. There was talk of putting me on one of the big registers, but Alejandro insisted that I should have an easier shift. Soon, I will graduate to where all the action happens and people buy massive racks of buffalo ribs and cheese that's been aged twenty years. Or at least that's what I imagine happens over there.

On express, I have more support around me. It's busy, but the item count is much smaller per person, so I can take the time to look up SKU numbers (inventory numbers) and not become overwhelmed. We all have to start somewhere, so they say, and why not in the belly of the beast, where hundreds if not thousands of customers come through each day—but only with ten items or less, so it's easier to learn?

Soon, Alejandro returns and says, "Are you ready?"

"Hell no!"

"Good! Let's do this."

* * *

Yesterday, I went on a grand tour of the Dream Grocers that is now my place of work. It's a store located in an affluent neighborhood with extravagant decor and ambiance at every turn. Towers of artisan cheeses and imported seltzer water sit under perfectly placed spotlights of soft-white lighting. Coolers are filled with lavish organic and locally sourced goods, placed there by seemingly anonymous faces that slip back into the shadows. Our produce shimmers in the gently falling mist of the immoderate conditions. We are in the middle of the United States, but the seafood department's selection has a freshly caught quality to it that comes only with being shipped by two-day-air. Our grocery aisles carry tiny one-hundred-dollar jars of manuka honey, hummus so fresh it will spoil in a hot car before you get home, and a general sense that you are walking through an art exhibit or a museum instead of a grocery store. And that's only what the customers can see.

Behind the walls and in the basement, a small army of employees utilize their arsenal of spices, raw meats, cake batter, icing, ovens, and mixers to create novel items for customers. There are dock workers receiving goods and employees counting and packaging items to put out on the floor. There is an unseen world working to support that sign on the front of the building and the chaos at the front registers.

As I walked the hallowed hallways full of people and processes you never see as a visitor, I tried to listen to my guide's instructions on what was what and where things were, but I found myself lost in thought more often than I was engaged with his instruction. I began to build this sneaking suspicion that I was witnessing something more profound than people gave it credit for, because this was how and where people built community.

It's a grocery cathedral of sorts where nutrition is burned in effigy. But in this subtle institution, there is far less worship and more participation in the production of sustainable human life than one might think. Maybe a more apt comparison is one of mitochondria—the people are the powerhouse inside of a cell. The workers behind the scenes make the whole thing function for the betterment of everyone.

Dream Grocers has been a staple of the lower east side of Denver for nearly thirty years. It's where all the oil barons and stockbrokers of my city come to shop for their groceries. In addition to the old money that resides in the area, our state is one of the most health conscious in the United States, so by extension, this place is one of the busiest yuppie pit stops you might run across. In orientation, Alejandro explained that not only do we have difficult shoppers to deal with, but our location is always competing for the top sales in our region. This particular store is a cash cow for the tri-state area.

I think I hear "Welcome to The Jungle" playing over the loudspeaker as a woman in a fur coat resembling the well-dressed Pomeranian tucked inside her purse drags along a desperate husband with a cartful of groceries.

From the few conversations I've had with employees and my own personal experiences in this particular store, I know that the customer base here isn't the easiest to deal with. But I don't see the deterrent in those facts. I'd like to think I'm a savage optimist, or maybe I'm just a secret masochist who feels the need to test the limits of what I'm capable of. Either way, I'm here, and there is no going back.

* * *

"Alright, man. Just wave down the next customer."

I feel like an idiot waving my hand like a fan of a famous rock band driving past in their tour bus, so I lean into it and wave harder. Alejandro and another cashier named Christian begin to laugh.

"I like the enthusiasm, but just wait until you meet some of these people. Sometimes it's downright disturbing."

"Yeah, dude. You might regret drawing attention to yourself like that."

A woman walks up to my line with a panicked and slightly confused look on her face. Her phone trembles in her hand. I ring up her items and tell her the total is fifteen dollars and sixty-two cents. Tears start to stream down her face.

"Are you okay?" I ask.

I don't mention that a police officer is on site at the store if she is in danger. It seems like a bold thing to say to someone.

She grabs a napkin out of her bag, blows her nose, and replies, "I just . . . I . . ." She is shuffling through her bag to find her credit card. "I'm so sorry . . . I just found out my brother died."

Her words hit me like a tidal wave—that feeling of "fight or flight" paired with empathy. What is one to do? Out of instinct, I ask, "What happened?" I immediately regret the question. "I'm sorry. That's none of my business."

"Oh no, it's fine. He was fighting cancer for over a year, and he just passed. I said my last words into his ear a few minutes ago."

As the computer processes her payment, she says, "I'm sorry. I don't mean to put that on you. I just, yeah . . ."

I don't know what to say besides, "I am so sorry for your loss. I . . . I . . . I hope you are going to visit family soon."

"I am heading to the airport after I leave here."

"That's good. Have a safe flight, and I hope you find healing together."

My words are cheesy, but she smiles and says, "Thank you."

"Whoa, that was heavy, man. You okay?" Alejandro asks.

"Yeah, I think I'm alright."

"That was a hell of a first customer to have."

I pause for a moment and look out on the floor. The humdrum of people scurrying about carries with it a sharp rhythm composed of customers talking, cashiers punching in SKUs, and baggers setting items in sacks. There is an undeniable and intimate electricity to the whole thing. I can see why people feel open to engaging employees—why they are willing to share their lives, even the painful parts, with complete strangers. This is where they acquire food to feed their families. It's a communal place and one of the only vestibules left where strangers weave their lives together in the real world.

"Alright, man. Let's get the next one up here," Alejandro says as I shake off my daydream.

* * *

People remind me of cattle kicking up dust in a corral as they shuffle into line. Their distinct facial expressions are full of modern concerns, like Norman Rockwell characters, as they glow in the light of their smartphones. They aren't looking so "bright" as I call for the next person in line. No one responds or even flinches at the request. I am six foot three, so I know that I'm easy to spot, but no one is paying attention despite the fact that their ultimate goal is to check out of the store.

"I can help who's next!" I say louder. Some people look up, but no one steps forward.

Alejandro is talking to another employee, so Christian, a coworker with dreadlocks and a devilish smirk, steps back and shouts, "Next!" and points to me. This shocks those in the line out of their transfixed states, and they begin to move.

"Thanks," I reply.

"No worries, man. You just gotta project," he says with a hearty laugh. "All of these Lindas and Daves are a bunch of dum-dums who never listen or pay attention. They forget why they're here. Sometimes I wonder if they even know we exist."

"Lindas? Daves?"

"Yeah, dude, this is a Linda-and-Dave world. Didn't you know that?" he says.

Another cashier named Neal leans back and says, "He ain't lying."

I try to save face for a moment but see no point and recant, "I don't get it."

"Here, help this next customer, and I'll explain," Christian offers.

I want to say something, but I see someone walking up before I can finish my response.

"Hello! How are you today?" I ask as I turn around, slightly flustered.

"I'm fine," the customer barks.

"Are you a Dream Team member?"

The shrewd-looking man leans toward my register without acknowledging my question.

I begin my spiel about how a Dream Team member is entitled to certain perks such as member-only deals and special discounts. My words make no impact on him as he peers at me with beady eyes through his round spectacles, then sets down a plastic container of nuts along with a few other items.

We are required to ask every customer about the status of their membership. If they aren't a member, we are supposed to encourage them to go online and sign up. But the door slams shut.

"How much are these cashews?"

It clearly states the price on the lid—$7.99 a pound. If one were to make an educated guess, they might say it is slightly over a half pound of cashews. I try the price-query feature, but it doesn't help clarify. I look for Alejandro to help, but he is nowhere to be found. Christian is busy with another customer. I try my best to figure out what the man wants.

"Well, they are seven ninety-nine a pound. I can't get an exact reading with the price query but—"

"You know what?"

I pause.

"I think they will be too salty. I don't want them anymore."

The label also states they are plain cashews.

"Oh . . . okay. But I don't think they are the salted kind."

"I will just take them back."

"You don't have to—"

He grabs the canister and walks away before I can tell him we could put them back later. I assume he will be right back. People stare at me while I wait for him to return.

He comes back to the register with the container still in his hand.

"These aren't the salted kind. Why didn't you tell me that?"

"Sir, I tried—"

"Oh, never mind. I need to get out of here."

"Okay. Well, your total is twenty-two dollars and eighty-nine cents, including the cashews."

"What the hell is that supposed to mean?"

"What is *what* supposed to mean?" I respond, dumbfounded.

"The cashews thing. Well, never mind. Hell, I don't want them. Here . . ." He grabs the cashews and walks away. Once again, I am left standing, awkwardly, without nuts as people watch this odd exchange. I remove the item from his bill and await his return.

The man walks up for a third time and aggressively shoves his credit card into the machine. "You know it's nothing personal, right?" he says.

I don't respond due to a fear of backlash.

"The cashew thing. It's nothing personal."

Sheepishly, I say, "Yes, I understand. Have a great day."

"You too," he fires back and storms off.

I look around. Christian smiles, holds up a big thumbs-up, and walks over to me.

"That type of shit happens all the time, man. You will get used to it."

"I guess I expected it. But, man, what a prick."

"He's a regular. You will see him all of the time. Just ignore Norman."

"His name is Norman?"

"Actually, I have no idea if that's his name. That's just what we call him. Norman is forever his name. Basically, he is just an older version of Dave that's more crotchety and entitled. His soul is a landfill crammed with missed playdates and twenty-five-year-old scotch. He hates his life even if he swims in luxury you could never understand, and at our store, he's the norm. We have Daves, Lindas, Normans, and the occasional outlier, but you can pretty much narrow down all the people you meet to those three names. They each bring their shit with them and lay it on your lap, but you will get used to it, I promise. Huh, Alejandro?"

I look behind me—Alejandro is back. "Yeah, man, Normans are the worst," he says as he grabs a grocery bag and props it open.

"Hey, buddy, where did you go?" I ask. "I could've used your help just now."

"Sorry, man. Didn't I tell you this is a constantly changing place? Any rules are so flexible they almost are nonexistent."

"Except I need to ask to take a break or go to the bathroom?"

He laughs and says, "Yes, exactly. But I'm sorry, man—they pulled me away. I'll try to stay here as much as I can, but I'm stretched pretty thin. Everyone here is. Our motto at Dream Grocers is 'Do more with less.' But look, you did great, and I am proud of you. Hell, we might move you to a big register today."

"Thanks, bro. Wait . . . what? I thought I would have a few shifts on the express to get myself acquainted with the job before you send me off to the big ones."

"That was my hope, and I fought for it, but like I said, everything here changes constantly. Most days it feels like I wander around in the fog of war, and I have no idea what register I'm on or who I'm talking to. This is a busy place. You'll see."

"Are you trying to scare me?" I ask sarcastically, but I'm truly a little worried.

"Nah, man. There's nothing to be scared of. Everyone here has experienced the fever dream. And they will help you through it all."

"Well, now I don't know what to think. You say all of the customers are assholes and I will be walking around in a fog of war every day with Normans or Lindas or whatever you call them haunting me with every move. That doesn't sound like the fun you described a little bit ago."

"Normans, Daves, and Lindas, oh my!" he says, and the whole crew breaks out in laughter. "You'll be fine, brother. Are all the customers jerks? Well, it's hard to say, but yes, for the most part. But personally, I think that the pet-name thing that Christian does is just his way of avoiding introspection about how he is a terrible person."

Christian leans over. "I heard that, asshole."

"But like I said in orientation. You get used to it. There is an ebb and flow to this whole place. It's like the ocean, ya know."

"Alejandro is such a goddamn hippie."

"That's rich coming from the guy with dreadlocks," Alejandro fires back. Then he looks at me. "Jesus, man, you look like someone just shit in your oatmeal."

"I feel like it," I confess. "All of these things you are telling me sound grueling. Now I'm not sure if this is the job for me."

Christian shakes his head. "We are just giving you shit, man. You're right. I'm not being fair, because not all of them are bad. In fact, I have some regulars I love and enjoy my conversations with, but I don't think it serves me, at all, to remember their names. This isn't a forever job, ya know, and I really try not to take work home with me."

"I see. So the pet-name denigration and fever-dream thing are a coping mechanism?"

"Sort of. Well, not the fever-dream thing. That's real, but it makes the days go by fast," Christian responds.

Alejandro puts his hand on my shoulder and asks, "Have you ever worked with the public before?"

"Well, yeah. Most of my life."

"Good. Then you know what's up. They just don't care. Hell, I'm not sure we exist to most of these people, even in passing. And if we aren't worthy of recognition, do you think they are? At least in this part of life. You know what I mean?" Christian explains.

"Yeah, I understand."

"Sorry, we shouldn't be so negative with you. It's been a long day," Christian says and begins to laugh. "Let's change the subject. Hmm . . . how did you get here? What's your story?"

"Oh, well, that's quite the shift and a loaded question."

"Nah, man. It's your story. Tell whatever part makes sense to you."

I realize now that we have been ignoring our line. Alejandro still has his hand on my shoulder like a wise uncle telling me the woes of binge drinking and public pools in the '80s. "Should we get back to some customers?" I ask.

"Oh yeah, good point. Are you sure you are doing okay? I want you to have a positive experience at Dream Grocers."

"Yeah, man. I get it. Look, I have been doing this type of shit most of my life. It's pretty much all I've ever known. Just on a larger scale. It's been a while since I've dealt with assholes face to face."

Christian points behind me, and Alejandro's eyes go wide as he covers his mouth, clearly trying not to laugh.

I turn around to see the face of Dave. "Oh, sorry! Hi, how are you today?" I say, hoping that he didn't hear what I had to say about assholes.

"I am doing fine. I just need a bag of ice, and here are the codes for two cups of coffee from the coffee bar."

I'm relieved he didn't notice my derogatory remarks. I ring up his items and move on quickly. My duties are simple, but everything feels hurried, because I don't know exactly what to do and the learning curve at my store goes at a heightened pace. The afternoon rush arrives, and we get too busy for anyone to fuck around. Or at least that's the way it feels. My conversation with Christian and Alejandro threw me off. Now I am thinking perhaps more than I should. I haven't held a public-facing job in years. I've occupied a cubicle for most of my adult life, and I wonder if I am ready for this brave new world filled with unapologetic, Botox-filled, neglectful parents and organic Tunisian mangoes.

* * *

It wasn't all that long ago that a gnawing pain in my leg oscillating between sharp and dull loomed as I sat at my desk. Every time I moved, fixed a spreadsheet, or answered a shitty email from a feeble mind who didn't understand punctuation, the metaphorical bear trap tightened around my leg. My only relief was the short walks back and forth to the kitchen or the bathroom like a dog pacing around in a dog run, imprisoned in some fool's backyard.

I would look down at my leg with uncertainty and disgust, then pick at the wound until it would bleed and fester. I found "self-care" through cocktails and cocaine or any other myriad of distractions. Year in, year out, I looked down at the snare around my leg and the chain that secured it. I'd even count the links. One thousand eight hundred and sixty-two dull, galvanized loops tethered me to a certain place or thing or idea.

The self-aggrandizing tragedies and pointless meetings one will endure to remain comfortable will leave you stupefied. And it could also make you wonder why people are so obsessed with the things that make them miserable despite the perks of security and privilege. The former should be canceled out by the latter.

You might not enjoy your work, but it affords you the luxury you desire.

Friends might scream at you to stop worrying about the "work" or "job," because those tasks don't define your life. But my response would be, "How can it not?"

You spend most of your waking life doing those tasks. They have to be part of your story. And that's why Christian's question has me thinking about what brought me to Linda, Dave, and Norman. And I realize now that the story I've been telling myself on how and why I got to this place is repetitive, bloviated, lengthy, and muddled because I never chose a path (as if there is such a thing) to go down. My friends must hate my circular stories and complaints.

I'd been falling forward my whole damn life, tripping on my shoelaces or not lifting my feet up, catching the uneven sidewalk over and over again, never considering my next steps. I'd acknowledge the shit holding me back, but I was surrounded by good people and all the resources I could have wanted. It was an easy life. I could numb that pain. And maybe that was why I found it suffocating more than liberating to have security.

No process ends in an instant. It takes time to break the chains you create for yourself, even if it's a specific conversation or circumstance that reveals the only option is to leave. My moment came in the late summer of 2019 as I was closing up shop on a hard day's work at a new job I was beyond excited to have in a company that was moving from California to Colorado.

The day was winding down at the corporate headquarters in San Francisco. I was finishing up my tasks for the day before I headed back to the hotel I had basically been living out of for three weeks. Everyone had already left besides my direct supervisor and one of my coworkers, Jamie. Earlier in the week, our supervisor told us that we should send her a recap of what we learned at the end of the week. Not my style but tolerable.

As I was packing up, I walked by her desk, and she inquired if I was leaving. I responded that I was, and she asked if I had sent my daily recap.

"Oh, I didn't know I needed to do a recap every day. Sure, I can send one."

"Yeah. I would just like to know what you are up to."

"Okay. Yeah, I'll send one to you."

I was surprised at her updated request. A daily recounting of tasks seemed like an overly tedious waste of time, and it set a precedent I found unnerving, but I went back to my computer and began to type up a summary of the day. A few minutes later, I looked down at the instant messenger window on my computer, and a new text from my supervisor read "I think you should think about how much you want this job. And you should be aware of how it looks to your new employers when you leave work early."

Slightly flustered and irritated, I responded, "Sorry, I didn't know that I needed to do a daily update. I am almost done with mine."

"It's OK. I just think it sets a bad precedent."

"That wasn't my intention. I just finished everything and didn't know I had to write a daily recap. Everyone was gone for the weekend. Anyway, I just sent the recap."

In that same moment, I received an instant message from Jamie saying, "Did you finish your daily recap?"

"Oh, she cornered you with that also."

"Yeah. I thought we only had to do a weekly recap."

"Me too. But yeah, I am about done with mine. Are you?"

"I'm getting there."

"Will you be able to make dinner?"

"Shouldn't be a problem. This is all very frustrating though."

"Couldn't agree more. Text me when you are done. We will all go to dinner together."

About a half hour later, when I got up from my desk to leave, I looked over toward my supervisor's desk and saw that she was gone for the night. She had left early, too, with only a passive-aggressive threat in tow. There hadn't been any clarification. Just an anxiety-inducing questioning of my dedication to the job.

I walked by Jamie's desk, where she was still working on her recap. She and I were going out to dinner later with another trainee. I didn't mention anything to her as I walked out into the chilled night air.

My nose began to run from the brisk crosswind of the bay as I walked down the street toward the hotel. I didn't want to go back to the confines of my hotel room yet, so I sat down on a park bench and stared across the bay at San Francisco and listened to the lapping of the waves.

The jacket I wore wasn't warm enough, but it didn't matter. I needed time to think. What the hell had just happened in there? That woman had just chastised me for nothing. I had traveled fifteen hundred miles to learn a new job as the company was set to move to Colorado, and I was met with a thinly veiled threat on my third week of "training." I was only a few weeks into my job and was being gifted with passive-aggressive messages about protocols I didn't know existed. I had just upended my life for a lecture on how to behave in her world.

San Francisco looked stoic, unmoved, and inspiring across the bay. The more I thought about that interaction, the more I had to fight the urge to take it personal. But I also wondered what I'd signed up for with this new position. That exchange had revealed my new manager's character in an unflattering light. Her need to control was obvious now. Passive-aggressive demands and comments don't inspire loyalty. They only fester and breed negativity. It had been an honest look into her soul and my place in that situation.

I knew this wasn't going to bode well for the prevailing anxiety I'd dealt with most of my life. On that windswept bench, I realized that, perhaps, I had jumped the gun on changing up my life for this particular job. Maybe I'd been overly excited to do something different and grand. I'd also wanted more money. I'd been pragmatic and myopic in my approach to my career. I dwelled on all of these things for a little while longer until my hands went numb, then I walked back to the hotel.

When I got back to my room, I lay on my bed, silently, in the dark, thinking too much and convincing myself that I had to push through and keep going. That I could put up with this shit for a while longer.

I looked at my phone. I had a text message from Jamie, who had experienced the same backhanded messages from our manager. The message read, "What was that shit all about?"

"No idea. That was incredibly unprofessional."

"I feel like she hates me."

"I don't think she hates you. I think she's a bad manager."

"I guess. I just feel like she picks on me."

"I kind of get that feeling too but she sent me the same bullshit. So, you're not alone. We just have to push through. Are you going out to dinner with me and Jenna?"

"Yeah. I don't feel like it though."

"It will help get your mind off it."

"Good point. I'll meet you in the lobby."

All three of us trainees went out to eat regularly. I enjoyed hanging out with them. We were a little crew learning to navigate a very new moment of transition in life. We would have drinks and laugh and chat about all manner of things. It was good fun, and it was on the company dime through our stipend for dinner when traveling for work.

That night we went to a ramen place in town. I drank Vietnamese beers and talked with the two women about the strange interactions with our manager, our futures, and the undeniably good food we were eating. I remember acting more positive about the situation than I actually was in my heart of hearts, and I tried to encourage Jamie. This was her dream job. For me, this was an opportunity, and that was all. Jenna fit in better with the new crew and had a more straightforward path. It was also her dream job, and she was well on her way to succeeding at the new job.

When Jamie, Jenna, and I got back to the hotel where we were all staying, Jenna split off for the night, leaving Jamie and I drunk and contemplative at the hotel bar, where we discussed how to proceed.

"I just don't know if this was the right decision," she said.

"Yeah. I was thinking the same thing. But once we get past the initial training, we will be home free, and she won't be a helicopter boss like she is now. We just have to get through this short period." I knew it was bullshit I was telling myself.

"Yeah. You are probably right," she replied.

We talked a little while longer, then went our separate ways.

Just a few weeks later, I looked back on that conversation and laughed at my silly resolve, because it had only gotten worse for me. From the get-go, something had felt off. My anxious nature had only worsened. I'd tried to explain to the manager, but she didn't have the capacity or empathy. I'd decided I needed to move on. I felt trapped in a corner that was partially of my own making.

My eagerness to make more money had landed me under the heat lamp of someone who needed to control and consume the things around her. I didn't actually care about the products we sold. It was strictly a job. It turns out I wasn't willing to put up with certain things. Thinking back on it now, I see that she may have been a Linda. It was her world, and I was stepping into it, ready to be pummeled and run out of town.

Eventually, the employees in our department stopped traveling back and forth to San Francisco. But that loaded conversation with our manager began the unraveling of a corporate life I half despised but needed in order to make ends meet. When the company had settled into our new digs in Denver, nothing changed. She only became more overbearing and aggressive in her management style. The us-versus-them mentality and the all-or-nothing bullshit was exhausting. I had to leave, and I did. Linda won that round. But I had no idea that I would be facing a different version of her almost daily in my next life.

This makes me wonder how many other times I have been dealing with Lindas throughout my life and I didn't even know it.

* * *

When I think of a Linda, I imagine her wearing a fur coat as she walks around a Walmart with her tiny dog. The little mutt has a serious viral infection that's contagious, but Linda doesn't care. In her mind, she exemplifies excellence, but in actuality she doesn't possess a single nice or meaningful thing, because everything she claims as her own is painted ugly by her abuse of others. She knows people, and she is known. Respect is expected but not earned, because she tried for a while and stepped on whomever to get where she is now. Continued effort to improve is not in her wheelhouse.

Linda is an idea. She is a caricature of unearned exceptionalism with the demand of a grizzled veteran. She is very American. Wide tastes with a narrow mind. Elite. Unsettling in the truth she reveals about the way we treat others in service positions. Linda is an unexamined life.

But in reality, Linda isn't like that.

"How are you doing today?" I ask Linda as she approaches my line.

"I'm doing good. How about yourself?" she responds.

I hate the lazy grammar in this conversation already, and I try to steer it in a better direction. "I'm doing well."

"Oh, good, good."

"Are you on the Dream Team?"

"Excuse me?"

"Do you have a Dream Team card?"

"Oh, I thought you said something completely different. I'm sorry. Yes. Yes, I'm a member." She pulls out her card, and I scan it.

"What did you think I said?"

"Never mind. It's silly."

"Okay," I respond and begin to ring up her groceries.

She has a flustered look on her face before she blurts out, "I thought you said, 'Do you want to scream?' And I thought to myself, 'Well, that's none of your business.' But that doesn't make much sense. Let's forget I even mentioned it."

"Well, do you want to?"

"Want to?"

"Scream. Because it's okay if you do. We are here for you at Dream Grocers."

Her eyes soften a bit, and she smiles, then continues to unload her groceries onto the conveyor belt.

I set some organic apricots on the scale, pause momentarily, and observe Linda, who has stopped loading groceries and started looking at her phone. I can see her screen. She is checking Instagram. Scrolling, scrolling, scrolling. And waiting for those likes to roll in for her. Lacking words to say, I laugh and enter the SKU for the apricots, 3201, and move on to the next thing to scan.

The following item is a six-pack of peach-flavored hard seltzers called Bench Press. I ask for the woman's ID.

She looks annoyed and puzzled at first, responding, "Umm, yeah, sure."

People get worked up over this all the time, so to ease her mind, I say, "Sorry, I have to card anyone that I think looks under forty."

With a gentle smile and a return of that blushed look, she says, "Oh, well, that makes sense."

I look at her ID. Linda Grayhaul-Troudeau, born August 23, 1980. *What the hell? Is this real?* Linda isn't just an idea. She is standing right in front of me. I look around as if someone might be connecting the same dots but quickly move on, considering that makes no sense.

Her fair skin hasn't aged well naturally. She has managed to spruce it up with the Botox and a possible face-lift. I can't be completely sure the face-lift happened, but it seems probable. The picture of her on the license is at least ten years old. She was quite beautiful, with more than a smirk of confidence radiating from her face. She was going straight to the top. This is only speculation, but something happened along the way that sent Linda right to where she is now.

I decide to start the conversation over and say, "Hi, Linda. Have any big plans for the weekend?"

"Oh yes, we are going to our lake house for the weekend. Boating, Jet Skiing . . . you know."

"Sure. Sounds like fun. But you know it's March, right?"

"Of course, silly. Our boat is at our place in Tahoe. No one can stay in Colorado all year long. At least I can't. I'd go insane. Do you know what I mean?"

"Sure," I lie. "Well, I am sure it will be a fun trip. I hope it's very relaxing for you."

"Gosh, I sure hope so. It's been such a long week."

I am nearing the end of her groceries, and people are lined up behind her, but I inquire, "Really? How so?"

"Well, my son is going through his terrible twos. He's so angry and violent all the time. And he always yells and screams and demands attention. I just don't know what to do."

"That sounds rough. Sorry, I wish I had some advice for you, but I don't have kids."

"Oh no. It's none of your concern. Our live-in nanny is really the one who should be worried. If things don't improve quickly, we might have to find someone new. And that would be a shame. I mean, Consuela is like family after all these years."

"I see. Well, have fun at the lake house," I say as I hand her the receipt.

She looks at my name badge. "Thanks, Dave."

"It's Daniel," I say under my breath.

"I'm sorry. Did you say something?"

"Yes. My name is Daniel. Not Dave."

"Oh, I am so sorry. My husband's name is Dave. I must have had him on my mind."

I can feel my brain cells pop like popcorn at the uncanny circumstance I find myself in as real-life Linda and Dave are married to each other in the real world and the sarcastic. She must notice my surprise.

"No problem at all. I am sure he is a great guy."

"Well, kind of—he is in here a lot, so maybe you will see him."

"Maybe."

She glances back at me for a short moment, but she checks out of the conversation and back into the phone as she continues toward the door.

Christian is walking by and stops for a moment. "Was that Linda?"

"Yes. How did you know?"

"She just had that look on her face."

"What look?"

"The kind that suffocates you with her perceived moral superiority."

"Damn. Yeah, and that was actually her name. And that description is freakishly accurate."

"Oh shit? Really?"

"Yup."

"I've been doing this for way too long. Not only do they look the same, but they are also the same. No matter the color or creed. Every one of them has that classic scowl on their faces. Wait until you meet some more Daves. They can be worse."

"That was her husband's name."

"No shit?"

"Yeah, I guess he comes in here all the time."

"Called it. How are you doing, man? Need any help?"

"Sure. If you want to bag, that would be awesome."

"No problem."

* * *

I imagine Dave in a completely different way from how I imagined Linda. If you want to call him *a man of substance*, you can, but really, he is a shell of the person he aspired to be. He's successful, sure, but he is a slave to the choices he made such as the wife he married or the career he chose. As a result, a touch of bitterness lingers in everything he does. He acts tough but is a pushover. He is weak willed, and that's why he and Linda work so well together. She runs his soft life. But again, he is elite in possessions and status. He knows people, and he is known. He takes out his dissatisfaction with life on people in the service industry. He is the epitome of projection—both subtle and obvious. Insecure and infantile, but he has won.

In the real world, Dave doesn't quite fit my expectations. A man walks up with a basketful of groceries. He has medium-length hair and dark-rimmed glasses. He looks at me briefly and begins to unload his cart.

"Hi, how's it going?" I ask. I see his mouth moving, but I can't hear what he is saying.

I lean closer and ask, "Sorry, I didn't catch what you said."

He pauses, looks at me, and then points to the earbuds that I hadn't noticed. As he unloads his stuff, I think, *Okay, great. I won't have to talk to this asshole*, and I start scanning his stuff. His conversation *must* be important.

I look over at Christian, and he nods. This must be one of the people he was talking about just a moment ago.

I place a few items in a bag, then look up to the man waving at me and pointing to a bag that he brought in himself. He takes out an earbud. "Yeah, babe, hold on—I am talking to the cashier."

"If you want to use your own bag, you will have to bag the groceries yourself," Christian says.

With an anguished look, the man says, "That's fine," and places the earbud back in. "So what I was saying . . ."

I'm smiling on the inside as I take all of the groceries out of the paper bag and place them on the counter. Christian walks over to the next register.

"Babe, seriously, calm down. I know you were just in here. I am sorry we missed each other. I will be home tonight. What? No, I am not cheating on you. Wait? Yes, I can grab you some crab cakes."

The next item I need to ring up is a six-pack of cheap beer. For the most part, we don't sell crap beer at my fancy store. I don't know where he found that shit, but he did. I need to ask him for his ID.

"Excuse me, sir . . . sir?" I ask with muted joy at the prospect of making him more annoyed.

He looks up again, seeming frustrated. "Yes," he replies.

"I need to see your ID."

"Fucking seriously?"

"Yup. It's the law."

"Hold on, babe. These assholes want my ID for the beer."

He pulls out his wallet and his ID. Dave Louis Troudeau III was born September 22, 1978. I pause to get a good look at this fuckstick whose *given* name is Dave, as though his parents *wanted* him to be a simpleton. His graying hair and light padding around the midsection tell me he's slipping from when he first bought that fancy Armani suit he is wearing. His shoes are scuffed, but overall he has the appearance of a high-end car salesman. Or maybe he's a middle manager at a financial firm where he has been hanging on for years as younger and more talented people pass him by.

"I'm sorry, sir. I can get fired if I don't."

"Whatever," he replies and asks, "Anything else I can get you? Oh, and I will be right back. I need to get my wife some crab cakes."

The line behind him is enormous. He ignores it and runs off.

I save his transaction and begin ringing up the next customer. I am halfway through the customer who was behind Dave when he gets back with wild eyes and a clenched jaw.

"What is this shit? I said I would be right back."

"I know, but I needed to keep the line moving."

"They've never done that before. Is this a new thing?"

Christian steps over. "It's standard protocol, sir."

"This is bullshit. Whatever."

I finish ringing up the other man; then I scan Dave's receipt and continue to ring him up.

"Sorry about that, Dave."

He ignores me. I am starting to plot my revenge.

"Well, now that I have you. Are you on the Dream Team?"

"Umm . . . what the hell is that?"

"It's our membership card, where you can get discounts or extra savings. Do you have the app on your phone, or is your phone number connected?"

"No, I don't have either, and I don't want that shit."

"Okay. No problem."

"I said I don't want the fucking dream whatever."

"Not a problem, sir. Please pay on the machine."

"Do you accept cash?"

"Not at this register. They are switching out my drawer right now."

"Jesus Christ, seriously, bro?" He points at the earbud again and says, "Babe. This is the worst place. Why do we come here? Like, what kind of operation are you running here?"

"Sir?"

"Here, just take my goddamn card."

"You have to put it in the machine."

He jams his card in the machine so hard that I think it's going to snap.

"That work?" he barks.

"Yup. Here is your receipt," I respond. I place his receipt in the bag and say, "Okay, Have a great day." He walks away.

Christian has an "Oh shit" look on his face as he walks over. "Man, that guy was pretty awful."

"Yeah, no kidding. I thought the express lane was supposed to be easy. And guess what?"

"What?"

"That Linda that walked through the line before him was his wife."

"No. Fucking. Way. I'm getting too good at this."

The next customer is staring at us as we chat away.

"Sorry, sir," I say in a panic.

Christian puts his hand up. "Sorry, sir. That was my bad."

"No problem at all. It's not like I had anything else to do."

We both look at each other and then back at the man.

"I'm just fucking with ya. We aren't all assholes," the customer says with a laugh.

"See, I told you," I say.

"I guess you were right. Every moment offers a different possibility. But let's chat later, dude. I'm done for the day. Good luck, and I'm telling you this place is a rat's nest of stories—both good and bad. And this will not be the last one you have to tell."

Chapter Two

A Linda I have seen on each shift walks into my line with a decadent purse in the top basket of the cart, where a child should be. A small girl sits in the large area of the shopping cart surrounded by groceries like a purchase about to be made. It's serendipitous in a tortured sort of way. I would try to joke with her if she didn't have a scowl etched into her face that looks like her date's credit card was declined after a caviar dinner.

Linda lifts the kid out of the basket, sets her on the floor, and begins unloading a wide array of items with reckless abandon while the little one tugs at her dress and twirls round and round. She doesn't look overburdened by motherhood; in fact, the child seems to be only a slight nuisance as she tells the little one to stop in a haphazard way.

I've learned a great many truths in my first few days as a grocery cashier. One being that you can come to understand someone by the way they unload their groceries from a shopping cart. The degree of sloppiness to which they are willing to present their selections to the cashier is one of the most obvious tells of their personal sense of worth. If they shovel their shit onto the belt for you to sort through, they are probably a shitty person. It's not the same as unloading quickly or in a disorderly fashion. I can understand not feeling a need to stay organized. I'm usually the same way. But it takes a special level of apathy to discard pile after pile of perfectly good food they are about to purchase on the conveyor belt like it's trash.

I go down my regular checklist of statements and questions: "Hi, how are you? Are you a Dream Team member? Did you bring your own bag with you?" I can probably guess the answers, but I'm robotic at this point in my shift.

For all three questions, I receive the same dismissive and muted response that has become her signature. The store is closing soon. My energy to care dissipates with every breath. I begin putting the items in bags.

Even with the fog of the day bearing down, I'm organizing each bag quickly, when suddenly, I hear her voice loud and clear say, "I'd like to leave this up here, if that's okay. Can you have someone grab a new one for me?"

I look up to see her holding a rotisserie chicken. *Goddamnit, not again!* She did the same shit the last two times through my line. A rotisserie go-back every fucking time. I stare for a moment. *Who returns a fucking chicken?* And three times, nonetheless. To add insult to injury, this particular chicken is leaking from the bag. *How does that happen?* Chicken juice is getting everywhere.

"Well . . . ?" she insists. I grab the bag and a towel to stop the leak. I want to take it out of the bag and throw one leg at her and one at the child, then shove the rest in her Louis Vuitton purse. It pains me to think she is raising that little one to be just like Mommy.

Flat faced and undeterred by her flippant attitude, I say "Sure" as I place the chicken on the register behind me.

The smell of butter and rosemary wafting through the air is distracting as I sort through her large order. The end of my day creeps closer as I hand her the receipt with hate in my heart and the smell of fresh rotisserie lingering in the air.

* * *

"Just the cookie?" I ask.

"Yup."

"Okay, great. That'll be one dollar."

I enter the SKU for the cookie and expect him to grab the little clear bag and walk away, but with a flipping of his fingers, he asks for an additional sack to carry it. I'm surprised by his lazy and laughable request, or maybe I'm a little more on edge than normal since it's the end of the day. I say nothing and put the cookie in a paper bag to appease my master.

"I'd like one with a handle, please."

Something irks me deep inside when he asks for a full-size bag to carry his fucking cookie. I roll my eyes as I reach down.

"What the fuck is that all about?"

Calmly, I respond, "I didn't say anything, man."

"Yeah, but you gave me a fucking weird look. I don't appreciate it. I have to walk, and I don't want to carry the cookie."

I decide to say nothing. The man isn't wrong. He has the vision of a hawk despite his dullard appearance. I'm usually excellent at disguising my neglected rage as typical grocery-store-clerk apathy. But my weary end-of-shift eyes must have revealed my disdain for his request.

In my imagination, I see him walking home or to wherever he intends to go while he eats his sugar circle and strolls down the sidewalk. There was no need to send additional trash with him. He smiles at the fact that he has an extra piece of paper to throw away. His achievement is substantial. Civility dies with every lumbering step. Here is where I write a short letter abridging our pain.

* * *

A pair of woman's hands tattooed with a crescent moon on one and the North Star on the other come into my view as she places all but one item on the check-out stand. "Do you have the mulberry-mint tincture in organic?" her voice rings out.

I look up to find a slender woman with manufactured dreadlocks wrapped into a bun over her head holding a glass jar of hemp balm in her hands. Startled, I reply, "Umm . . . I—"

"I looked around, and I couldn't find the mulberry-mint one," she interrupts.

I make an executive decision. "We are out of that one for now. I think we are out of the juniper-lemon scent too. That one is my favorite," I lie.

She pauses for a moment, looks satisfied, and sets the balm on the conveyor belt. "I guess this will have to do. My customers will not be happy, but I think it smells lovely."

"What kind of business do you own?"

"I don't know if I would call it *my* business. My customers are the owners, and we are a community."

"Ah, I see . . . well, what kind of business do y'all own?"

"It's a holistic-health-and-wellness business. We strive to heal our bodies and souls through Mother Nature's gifts rather than the Big Pharma bullshit."

"Oh cool. So you are a nonprofit."

"Oh god no. I need to make a living. We just make decisions together, as a group."

"What's the name?"

"The Natural Solution."

"What are you trying to solve?" I reply.

"Excuse me?"

I pause for a moment, wondering how that question could possibly be confusing, and realize she is not what we might call a "deep thinker" and laugh.

"What is so funny?"

"The absurdity of it all."

"Of my business?"

"Well, no. Just life in general."

"I don't get it."

"Never mind. It's an inside joke."

"Do you think that's appropriate with customers?"

"Is what appropriate?"

"Making inside jokes."

"It wasn't a . . ." I trail off. "It wasn't an insult, if that's what you were thinking. I was thinking of a few things at once."

"It's fine. We take The Natural Solution very seriously."

"As you should. Where is your studio, if you don't mind me asking?"

"My studio is just down the street in a beautiful high-rise. We overlook the city while we meditate and chant our mantras."

"Sounds interesting."

"You should join us."

"Yeah. I think I could do that. How much is it?"

"Fifty dollars per session."

I nearly choke on my own spit. "Yeah. That's a little out of my price range," I say with a shrug. Like what does she think I do for a living, and how much does she think I get paid? I feel insulted for a moment, but then I look into her soft, empty eyes and realize she's not with me in any sense of the word. This is small talk. I'm being patronized. And it's not really her fault.

"Well, how about I give you a free pass, and you can see if you like it?"

"That's mighty generous of you."

She smiles and replies, "Of course."

She hands me a piece of paper that reads "One FREE admission to The Natural Solution with the purchase of a Natural Solution yoga mat."

I look up as the woman is leaving. She says, "Have a great day! See you soon."

I wonder how she justifies charging unnatural prices for her "Natural Solution." She utilizes capitalism and the free market yet says she isn't the owner of her studio. It's a communal space where all the patrons make the decisions. Do they all want that specific balm? Did they communicate the need for specific items from the grocery store and then vote on the ones that should be chosen? Something inside of me says NO as she walks away with her Gucci bag and UGGs. I don't fault her for thinking in a certain manner in which she both rages against and fully embraces the framework that helps her succeed. I'm just curious as to how she gets swallowed up by cognitive dissonance. And I wonder the same about myself. Maybe I am the one missing the point here.

* * *

This day seems impossibly long, and I'm searching for social relief through all forms of actions, ranging from flirting to just messing with people. That's half the reason I got this job. I'm undeterred by the pinch of shame I think I should feel with an admission of what some might consider sleazy motivations. But I never ask for a phone number. Actually, the word *flirt* doesn't accurately describe the interactions I have with the women who have crossed my path so far. From my perspective, they primarily consist of silly, conjecture-filled conversations with passing enjoyment.

A warm, soft regard is a good sign of a potentially fun conversation, and when she walks into my line, her beautiful brown eyes pull me in like gravity. She seems dutifully at ease in her own skin with a confident smile and swagger. It's driving me wild. I want to know everything about her, but we have only a few moments.

"Can you take this card back for me? I decided not to get it."

"Really? I think it's awesome," I say as I examine the card with the words "Your Birthday" followed by the images of a person doing a karate kick, a plus sign, and a donkey. It's a clever little card. "I mean, birthdays kick ass. So it gets right to the point."

"Well, I don't know. I guess I just like the other one more," she replies with a shrug.

The other card has an ice-cream cone filled with jewel-studded rainbow soft serve on the cover. I examine it slowly and look up at her, trying my best to smile with confidence when I'm actually a little bit nervous.

"Oh, come on!" she pleads playfully.

"I mean, it's not bad. But the kick-ass card is waaay better."

"Oh, whatever."

I laugh to reaffirm that I'm teasing and put the kick-ass card on the go-back pile.

"Do you really not like this one?"

"It's great," I reply as I motion for her to lean in. While pointing to my chest, I say, "It doesn't really matter what the card says. It matters what's in here."

The tops of her cheeks lift as she smiles from ear to ear, and we both laugh in unison. I hand her a bag with groceries and a receipt and say, "This is where I leave you."

"For now," she says.

* * *

40

He is methodical in his approach to checking out. The items are organized on the belt in a particular manner so he can place them in their proper spots in his rugged thermal bags. Cold will go with cold, produce with produce, hot with hot, and so on. I have seen this time and time again today, but after the normal pleasantries, I decide to ask, "So if you don't mind me asking, what do you do for work?"

"I don't mind at all, but is there a particular reason you're asking?"

"Oh, just how organized you are. Honestly, it makes my life much easier when people organize their groceries like you did. Especially when I have to bag."

"Interesting. I'd be surprised people would be that organized, then have you bag their groceries."

"Yeah. I am new to the job, but it seems most people would rather just watch me bag the items while they dive into Instagram."

He laughs. "How long have you been working here?"

"It's my first week."

"Damn. This place must get kind of overwhelming with how busy it gets."

"It's pretty crazy. But I'm just going with it. It's kind of fun, actually. I'm meeting interesting people left and right."

"Ah, well . . . I am glad to hear that, and you're doing a great job."

"Oh, thanks. Now, what do you do for a living?"

"I'm a brain surgeon."

"No shit! What hospital?"

"Ridgeline Memorial."

"Oh, well, that's very cool. It's not every day that you meet a brain surgeon."

"I guess that's true." He smiles as he puts the items in his bags in an organized way.

"And I'm glad you are organized, since you are poking around inside people's skulls for a living."

"Yeah, I probably need to know where I am going and what I am doing."

"This is true."

I am just now noticing that he has a huge amount of groceries packed neatly on the conveyor belt. He is walking back and forth between bagging and loading groceries. He is a machine.

"Man, this is a ton of groceries. You stocking up for a while?"

"No, this will probably only last us a week."

"Oh, wow! How many kids do you have?"

"Six kids. About a year and a half apart each."

"My god," I blurt out without thinking.

He pauses for a moment and gives a hearty laugh. "I know, right? I have been a busy man since my early twenties."

"Ahh . . . good for you. Kinda makes me wonder what I am doing with my life. I'm in my early thirties, single, childless, and working at a grocery store."

"Well, are you happy?" he asks.

I'm surprised by his response. "Actually, yeah. I'm writing a novel," I say in defensive mode.

"Oh really! That's amazing. I don't think I could do that."

"Ha. You're too busy with brain surgery."

"Well, yes, in a way, but I'm jealous of your creativeness. It doesn't work like that for me. I started on a road a long time ago, and I stuck to that path through thick and thin."

"Like you came out of the womb stitching and thrusting?"

He laughs. "Exactly. But really. I wanted this life from an early age. And I got it. We all have a different approach. But some people—in fact, most people—don't have a linear trajectory at all. For most folks, life is more like a quilt, and they add patches along the way. But they never finish the quilt. So if you are happy, you're good to go."

"Brain surgeon and a philosopher."

"Just think about it."

"For sure. Thanks. Well, here is your receipt, my good man. Have a great day."

"You too," he responds and begins to walk away.

As my mind jettisons off, my view turns wide, taking in the hustle and bustle of the front end; I think back on my response to the brain surgeon's question about me being "happy" and how it wasn't my finest moment, and immediately, I'm bogged down by self-doubt. Sure, I'm "writing a novel," but I've been doing that for over ten years. I have scraps and pieces and ideas, but I don't know what I should write about. I don't have a story. The "novel" seems like more of a metaphor at this point. And *happy?* What the hell does that even mean? I guess I'm happier than before, but what is the point of the word or feeling if it's all relative? And then it hits me—I'm floating, like a rudderless fool with a chip on my shoulder, going with whatever current hits my life next. This can't be the place I am supposed to be. My view begins to narrow. The customer is staring at me. He must have said something. I begin to panic.

A moment passes; I take a breath and start my standard greeting, but the new customer is looking behind me. I turn around to see the brain surgeon strolling back.

"What's up, man? You forget something?

"Just that I wanted to tell you . . . you are right where you need to be."

Chapter Three

Iabsentmindedly scan the first bag of king crab legs. The price shows up as $95.34. I know they are expensive but think nothing of it until she hands me another package of king crab legs with $80.69 on the label. "Damn, you guys are going all out on the crab leg, eh?" I blurt out.

Linda gives a hearty laugh and responds, "Well, they want only the best for special occasions."

"Who is 'they'?"

"Oh . . . my kids."

"Those are some lucky kids."

"No kidding. I mean, back when I was a kid, we started out with snow crab legs. But kids these days. All they want is sushi and king crab legs."

"What's the occasion?"

She starts laughing. "Well, one of the kids got an A in Statistics III this quarter. So she should be all set to get into Harvard now . . . and honestly, it really is a celebration for all of us. We worked so hard to get her into that school, and she almost fucked it up. We don't tolerate failure at our house."

"That *is* quite the occasion. How old is she?" I say with a heart full of sadness for that young girl.

"She is thirteen."

I cough and say, "My god. That's so young."

"I know, and she worked so hard. We are proud of her. Especially with everything going on in the world, you know?"

"The world is definitely a scary place," I respond.

"Yeah. The schooling has taken a toll on our social lives."

"I guess we all have to make sacrifices, right?"

"Too many, if you ask me."

"I'm sure she will get into the school of your dreams," I mumble as I hand her the receipt. "Enjoy the crab legs."

It's time to go on my fifteen-minute break. I call a supervisor to get some relief. I'm not sure I can survive another Linda. They are needy vultures picking at my time and emotions. I'm wearing thin.

The next person is getting in line. No one is answering the phone. Shit, it's a Linda. I don't need another one of these ghouls at the moment. The phone continues to ring, and I give up and turn around to greet the customer.

* * *

I find no relief from the onslaught of patrons when I return to my register after my break. They are still lined up with fierce looks in their eyes. When I reach the front end of the store, another supervisor named Mike walks up to me and says, "Hey, dude, we are going to put you on a big register. You okay with that?"

"Umm . . . sure. Is there anything I need to know about it?"

"No. You will need to look up more codes for produce. But it's nothing major, and you can ask for help. I only need you to do it for a few hours anyway. Your shift is over soon anyway, right?"

"Yup. I am off in two hours."

"Okay, perfect," he replies.

* * *

The next person in my line is distractingly beautiful as she unloads a cart with groceries overflowing. I keep mistyping the necessary SKUs into the system, and it's taking a very long time to finish her order. Neither of us mind. She walks to the end of the register to start bagging. I am mesmerized by her natural inclination to help. She carries with her the swagger of someone in complete control—a person who enjoys only the confines of her choosing. I slide into a conversation.

"Let me guess; this is only a week's worth of food?"

She laughs and says, "You guessed right."

"How many kiddos?"

"Well, I have three kids, but I also own a day care. Some of this is for them."

"Sounds like you have your hands full."

"Honestly, I'm at the best place I've been in years. My ex is gone."

There is a flicker of hope in my soul.

Unsure of how to respond, I ask, "Oh yeah?"

"Yeah. He tried to take everything from me for years. I'm so glad it's over."

"Years?"

"All the way back to my nightclub days."

"Umm . . . what kind of clubs? Brass poles?"

I fear these words the moment they come out of my face, but she covers her mouth and cackles. "No, no . . . not *those* kinds of clubs. I worked as a bottle-service manager as a side hustle for years. A side hustle before I started the day care."

"Daaamn . . . you win the award for most interesting customer today. So you ran the day care and worked at night selling bottles of alcohol to rich assholes?"

"Yup."

"You know . . . what is your name?"

"My name is Jennifer."

"Well, Jennifer, my name is Daniel, and now that we have developed a subtle yet genuine rapport, may I ask you something?"

"Of course."

"Will you marry me?"

She bursts out in laughter and says, "Well, there's one issue."

"What is it? Is it my hairline? I can get plugs."

"You're hilarious. No, that's not it. I mean, love takes time, Daniel. If I am going to spend the rest of my life with you, we need to have at least three exchanges at your register."

My heart sinks. She can see it.

"So shall we reconvene again soon?" she says in the most loving of tones.

I finish ringing up her groceries and place the receipt in her angelic hands. In return, she hands me a piece of paper. My heart begins to flutter. "Have a good night," I say as I begin to melt in anticipation.

"You have a good night too."

The grocery store is a runway as she walks toward the door, and all the world lies at her feet. I stare, drool, wish, and then I come back to earth. Another customer is unloading their groceries onto the belt.

My hands are sweaty as I open the paper from our exchange. Out of the darkness of a long, strange night, I see hope in the form of a lipstick kiss on a paper with "I almost said yes" written underneath. I don't know whether I should cry or laugh. I wonder when she had time to make such an elaborate note. I was looking at her almost constantly during our time together. Does she have a sticky pad full of these in her purse for emergencies? Something inside of me doesn't care. Maybe I will see her again, but most likely that spark was all we had.

* * *

When I look back, another woman is in my line, and she is already putting her credit card in the machine. I begin to ring up her groceries.

"Hello, how are you doing today?"

I don't receive a response. The woman isn't looking at her phone. But she is looking at her daughter and not talking. The little girl is holding a little shih tzu in her arms.

I try a different approach. "Hi, ma'am, are you on the Dream Team?"

Again, nothing. No acknowledgement of my person.

"What does he want, Mommy?" the little girl asks her mother.

"I don't know, honey, but I guess they expect *us* to talk to *them*. Listen, baby, set Daisy down. Make sure not to let go of the leash."

The moment the little girl sets the dog down, it starts barking.

"Why would you talk to them?" the daughter replies.

"I don't want to, but I guess I am supposed to, baby. We should remember that."

She turns to me and says, "I don't know what Dream Team you are talking about."

The dog continues to bark.

"It's our reward program—"

"Oh, I'm not interested. So are you done yet?"

I look down at the conveyor belt full of groceries, and I don't have anyone available to help bag groceries. "It'll be just a few more moments."

The dog continues to yelp. People behind her are staring. But she doesn't seem to care—or be aware of the situation, for that matter.

The child picks up the shih tzu, but it does not stop the animal.

Beep . . . beep, bark, bark . . . beep . . . look up and enter SKUs 32560, 68912, beep . . . beep, bark, bark. The line of groceries and the people behind her seem endless as she shuffles around impatiently and stares at me with disdain. She puts her hand on her hip.

"Seriously, baby. Keep your dog quiet."

"She won't stop, Mommy."

"Goddamnit. Give the dog here."

The little girl is crying as she hands over the dog. Daisy continues to bark.

"Sorry it's taking so long," I say.

"It's fine. We can't all be good at something."

"No, we can't."

"What is that supposed to mean?"

"Nothing important. Here is your receipt."

"See, honey, this is why we don't talk to these people." And with the little girl crying and the mutt barking away, they walk out the door. I hope they all die in a car crash on the way home.

* * *

A young couple steps into the line and unloads their basket. He says something, and she giggles. They both look over at me.

"Hello, how are you? Are you part of the Dream Team?"

The guy looks over at me and says, "Nah, bro, we aren't."

I begin to scan groceries and go about my business. I catch her looking at me while whispering in his ear. He proceeds to glance over at me. The young woman leans over and asks, "Have we met you before?"

"I don't think so. But I have been told that I have one of those faces by many people."

"Are you sure?" she replies.

"Yeah. I'm pretty sure."

"Okay. You just look so familiar."

"Where do you think you know me from?"

"Honey . . . did we meet him at the Halloween party?" she asks the oversize man with tiny legs and a huge back, chest, and neck.

"Nah, babe. I don't think so."

"Baby, I think we did."

"Nah. It's not the guy."

"How can you be so sure, baby?"

"That guy did not work at a grocery store. He had a real job."

"I think it's the guy."

"I don't care. It's not."

"Don't talk to me like that, Davey."

"It's Dave, babe."

"Don't call me *babe*. Not now. Not ever."

"Listen, I'm sorry. This could be the guy from the party, but I don't think it's him. I am sorry."

"It's alright, baby. I don't know either. It's just that he has similar eyes. But you are right. I don't think that guy would have worked a shit job like this."

"That's what I was thinking. Still, I'm sorry, baby. You know that you're my one and only, Lindy," he says.

"And you are my one and only, Davey." She opens her arms, and he leans over. "I forgive you. I love you so much."

"I love you too, baby."

"Give me a kiss."

He proceeds to pull her in and jam his tongue down her throat. "Davey" cups her butt, and one hand slides inside of her shorts. I watch for a moment.

"Excuse me. Hey, guys . . . you are all set. I just need you to pay."

They are undeterred.

A woman behind them chimes in with, "Hey, lovebirds! Some of us have places to go and shit to see besides your public fuck session."

The couple looks back at me, and Davey says, "What did you just say, dude?"

"I didn't say anything, man. That was a customer in the line."

"Sure sounded like you."

"Wasn't me, sorry, but are you ready to pay?"

"Sure, man." He moves to pay. "You're lucky I don't kick your ass right here."

The girl pulls him back. "Baby, I don't think it was him."

His finger is in my face. "You're lucky my girl is here."

"Here is your receipt. Have a great day."

He flips me off as they walk away, and then he yells, "Fuck you!"

The woman behind them walks up and says, "I'm so glad you told them to fuck off."

"I thought you said that."

"Not a chance. Maybe it was someone farther back in line. Either way, they deserved it. I hope they don't come back and retaliate."

"We can only hope," I say with blazing apathy.

"Oh wow! Look at that guy over there," she says as she points at a man holding a stack of steaks in cardboard trays while walking in the prepared-food aisle. "Some people just don't have any common sense."

"I guess you are right. Oh, look . . . that nice fella just set a few steaks into a wall cooler with green beans and house-made meatballs in it. Guess you were right to judge him."

"Do you want me to say something to him?" she asks with clenched fists. She begins to tremble and turn red.

"Nah, it happens all of the time."

"Seriously, I will say something."

"It's all good. In fact, I see a grocery employee picking them up now."

"I would never do something like that. I try to treat people with respect."

"That's good."

"No, seriously. I have worked a shit job like yours before. I think you people deserve respect."

"Aww . . . thanks."

"No problem."

"So your total is one hundred fifty-six dollars and ninety-four cents."

"Holy shit! Did you ring up some things twice?"

"I don't believe so."

"Let me see the receipt. I think you rang up some items twice."

I pause for a moment, thinking she can't possibly be serious, but she stares at me, so I give her a printout of the receipt.

She examines the paper closely. "This can't be right," she says in an exasperated tone. "Those steaks were not twenty-six dollars apiece."

I pull the items out of her bags and point to the price tags. They were twenty-six dollars apiece. She looks closely and says, "I think they were on sale."

"Well, I can knock a few bucks off of them."

"Yes. Please do."

"Sure. How about four dollars off apiece? So they are twenty-two dollars apiece. Actually, I am allowed to take ten dollars off your total purchase. I will do that."

"That sounds great."

"Okay. Great. Your new total is one hundred forty-six dollars and ninety-four cents."

She pauses for a moment. "You know that still sounds like way too high of a total." She examines the receipt more.

The other patrons are growing restless. I watch her peer at the piece of paper as if she can change the total with her eyes. After what seems like ten minutes, she looks up and says, "You know, I think I am going to leave the steaks with you. Can you take them off the total?"

I look at her for a moment, then look toward where the other man left the steaks he had been carrying. They are long gone. "Sure. I can do that for you."

"Thanks. I didn't realize you all are so expensive. Maybe you could talk to your manager about lowering some of these prices."

"Yeah, I will mention that to them."

"Thanks. I really appreciate that."

"Have a great day."

My replacement arrives and asks, "Are you ready to go home?"

"Oh man, am I ever?"

I grab my stuff and get out of my register as quickly as I can. "Thanks. Have fun," I say to my replacement. He smiles and begins checking people out.

The store is still teeming with all walks of life trying to get what they need as I walk by and head upstairs to the time clock. After I punch out, I see Alejandro walking past. "How'd your fourth day go?" he asks.

"Huh? It's only my third day, man."

"What? No, it's your fourth," he insists. "I was off yesterday, and we were training on the register the day before."

"What? That was yesterday," I say as my confusion grows.

Alejandro laughs. "No, dude, you were on express most of the day. Today you were supposed to be on a big register. Were you on one?"

"Well, yeah, I was."

"See, there you go."

I give him a confused look.

"The Fever Dream Grocers already got you, huh? I told you, man. This place will confuse you so quick."

"I guess so. I need to get home."

"Have a good night, man."

"You too," I reply and walk down the stairs.

I walk by the customer-service desk, and the lady who returned those steaks is pointing to her receipt again, but this time she has rage in her eyes. The supervisor, Mike, looks like he is giving in to whatever demand she has raging through her head about what was too expensive this time. She might be getting more items refunded—or she is demanding free things. Who knows?

I walk out the door, jump onto my bike, and ride out into a bleak spring day with a rust-colored sky and an odd stillness to the city as the sun sets behind apartment buildings and trees. The amber of a new phase of my life glows on my face as I churn my legs faster and faster and the cold spring wind rips past me.

Chapter Three

***

I arrive home trampled and worn thin physically but renewed in spirit. I was yelled at, flirted with, and leveled in a way I didn't expect, because I came to my job as a cashier after spending a decade doing shit I hated. It's not as if I'm forced to do this line of work. I made a conscious choice. It's easier to see the positive in an experience when you walk into it on purpose.

Out on my section of sidewalk on the three-story walk-up, I sip on some whiskey and ice. My neighbors, Jason and Levy, are sitting on the community patio drinking cocktails.

"Hey, dude, how was work?" Jason asks.

"It was lovely."

"Lovely?" he says with a laugh. "Really?"

"Yeah, in some ways."

"In what ways?"

"Well, for one thing, it's the first time in years that I don't feel obligated to take my work home with me. Like I left that shit at the door."

"Oh yeah! I forgot you came from a corporate gig that you hated."

"Exactly. I also made some headway with a beautiful woman today."

"Did you get a phone number?"

"No. I wish."

"Ah, well, I wouldn't count on that going anywhere," Levy says.

"Why not?"

"Well, a virus might wipe us out," Levy replies.

"What virus?" I ask.

"Didn't you hear? The coronavirus hit our state today."

"Ohh . . . no shit?"

"Yeah, man. It's crazy. They are saying deaths will be in the millions," Jason interjects.

"Well, that's terrifying."

"I know. That's why we are drinking."

"I'll cheers to that," I inform them.

As we lift our glasses, Jason puts his hand up. "Dude, hold on. Can you guys hear that?"

"Yeah. What is that?" I ask.

"The neighbors are fucking," Levy replies with a snicker.

"No, no, that's someone crying," Jason says.

"Damn, dude. I think you're right. That's some loud crying."

We settle into the silence for a moment, and the noise escalates. What was light sobbing is now full-on wailing. I look around to see where it is coming from, but it must be bouncing off the walls. The city seems unusually quiet. The only sound now is the clinking of ice in a glass as Levy pours another cocktail and the deep howls of distress coming from an unknown building.

"Should we call the cops?" I ask.

"On what and to where?" a voice responds. I'm distracted and buzzed.

We all look at each other and shrug and take a drink.

"So what happened with this woman at work today?" Jason asks.

"It's hard to talk about that when I can hear someone crying."

"Good point." And as he responds, the crying stops, followed by a muffled conversation.

"Can you make out what they are saying?"

"I think so. I'm pretty sure it's a woman."

"What is she saying?" I ask.

"She is saying something about their honeymoon?"

"I can hear her now," Levy says. "Sounds like they are canceling their plans. Her fiancé is trying to console her."

"Where are they going?"

"Jamaica, I believe."

"Nice," Jason says with a drunken smile on his face.

"Now he is saying something about how they are going to make it together."

"Oh, now here comes the sex."

"Maybe . . . wait." Levy motions to stop talking with his hand.

"Come on, man. Tell us. I can't hear beyond the rim of my cocktail glass."

"They are just really sad because they were looking forward to the trip more than the wedding."

"And now they are cooped up together for months with nothing to look forward to," Jason observes.

"Exactly. You look like you need a refill," I say.

"Sounds reasonable."

We are all pretty intoxicated now, and I feel relaxed with a day full of action behind me and good friends in front of me. I'm glad she stopped crying. The crisp spring air hangs heavy with change. But what kind of transformation are we in for? I worry about this virus news and ask, "What do you think of the virus news?"

"I think it's gonna be alright, man. It doesn't sound super serious, and everything I am reading online indicates that we should be out of the woods in six months."

"That's a long time," I reply.

"It'll fly by," Jason says with a chuckle.

"Somehow I doubt that."

"Is there anything left but doubt?" he says.

"I don't know. You tell me."

"Sorry, I didn't think of an answer. I thought of it as more of a reciprocal question."

"You mean rhetorical."

"Sure." Jason laughs again. I am thinking we should head to bed.

"Maybe we should call it a night?"

"I don't doubt you on that."

"Good. Let's stay positive here."

"That's all we can do."

"See you guys later," I say as I saunter back to my apartment.

The remainder of my night is spent scrolling through Twitter. Cases rising. People on high alert. Blame being thrown in every direction. Division being seeded. Men and women stand on towers made of egos as thin and fragile as a mountain of stained glass. Too much information for any sane person. It's impossible to look away.

I clear out another glass of whiskey as my eyes water from the glow of my smartphone. Shadows dance from the windows of my neighbors' apartments. Looks like sleep is in short supply tonight. A counter on my phone increases as more cases are reported. Conspiracy theorists claim inconsistencies. Politicians reassure us of their importance to our safety. Something feels off, but

I'm listening and reading and digesting what I can with the hair on the back of my neck standing on end as I watch chaos ensue. The light fades out—or maybe it's my mind. The sun will be up soon. And what that will look like has never been more unclear.

Chapter Four

By the time clock, a white board looms with dark handwriting on it that reads, "Attention Dream Grocers team: Information coming soon. Please check with your supervisors for any updates."

"Was that board there before?" I ask an odd little man who seems startled that I am talking to him.

"I don't know," the man replies.

"Weird. I've never seen it before," I reply as I turn toward him, but he walks away without saying another word.

"Doesn't really help, does it? And it's far too vague," Christian says as he walks up. "Our store managers are nowhere to be found. Some people said they are skipping town." He begins to laugh.

"Skipping town? That's absurd. Why would they do that?"

"Fear of the masses. Fear of what we might do?"

"What might we do?"

"I don't know, but the tension is real. People might get desperate."

"Jesus, that's pretty dark."

"You know me. I like to stay positive."

"Always."

"How are those stories stacking up for you?" Christian asks.

"Shit man. This place is wild."

"It's definitely a trip. Aaand there is a virus coming."

"I know, man. I stayed up all night reading about it."

"I think the whole world did."

I imagine billions of tiny screens in a dot-matrix spread across the dark side of our lonely planet as we scream along an infinite and exposed path. Solar flares and asteroids whiz by our silly ball of mud and ego all the time. Birth and death are happening at every moment. We are in bed with our extinction, nuzzled in its embrace, and we don't even know it. Or we do know, but we choose not to acknowledge the frailty of our situation. It takes the advent of social media and a microscopic enemy to bring our inevitable end to light.

"I guess I can take comfort in that," I respond as I shrug.

"In what? That you aren't alone?"

"Yeah."

"I wouldn't."

"Why is that?"

"Because, in the end, you are alone."

The pattern of illuminated faces spread across the world either brings us together or it isolates us forever.

I can't decide. Maybe I'm embracing the melodrama a little too much and sinking away from my humanity.

I laugh. "We should call you Christian the Positive."

"I like the ring of that. Are you headed home?" he asks.

"Nah. Just getting here."

"We are always like ships passing in the night," Christian responds.

"Yeah, dude. I rarely work with the same people. I don't know most of these folks."

"Well, it's your first week. You will get to know them," Christian reassures me.

"Do you know everyone here?"

"No. Most people don't work here long enough."

"How long have you worked here?" I ask.

"Three months."

"That's it? You're a sage of the grocery world."

"It's the dreadlocks and the marijuana edibles. They make me seem mature and affable," Christian says with a laugh.

"Must be."

"But really, this place is for the in-between times. I run my own business, and this helps me pay for the time in the gaps."

"Are you going to work here much longer?" I ask.

"I'm not sure. Probably not."

"So that's why you aren't worried about the lack of information or the leadership leaving."

"I'm worried about all those things."

"You don't seem like it."

"When you see enough of this place, you will understand. It flattens your nerves. Shouldn't you be heading down to the front?"

"Oh shit! Yes, I'll talk to you later."

* * *

Linda's shopping cart is piled high today with cans of green beans, pinto beans, white beans—all the beans—artichoke hearts, tomatoes, olives, corn, and tomato sauce and other nonperishables such as rice and shelf-stable almond milk. She loads the items onto the belt, and I begin to scan.

"So what's with all the cans? Feeling the pandemic paranoia?"

"Oh, a little bit, but this is mainly for my boss. He is worried we are going to be quarantined for months."

"What does your boss do?"

"He is a dentist."

"A dentist, you say?"

"Yeah, and I wonder what's going to happen too. Seems like the cases are growing really fast on the West Coast."

"If a dentist is paranoid, maybe I should be too."

We laugh together, but I'm starting to think it's not just talk, given that people are reacting to this thing already.

Our interaction is pretty simple, and she seems friendly, so I ask, "Why would a dentist be prepping for the virus?"

"Well, oddly enough, he has a background in epidemiology. And he is very concerned with how the government is going to respond to the virus."

"Is he worried about the virus himself?"

"Yes. I mean, he is in his sixties, so he has some serious concerns."

"Ah, well, that makes sense."

"Yeah, and it looks like the rest of these people are thinking the same things," she says and points to the growing lines.

"Well, here you go. Stay safe." I hand her the receipt.

"You stay safe too." She walks away.

I look back at the lines of people frothing, bursting with groceries—impatiently waiting for their turn to check out. Their mannerisms are limited and tense. The carts are piled high like people are shopping for Thanksgiving. Was it this busy all day? Sometimes I fall into a flow state that combines bullshitting with people and ringing up groceries, and time flies.

"Hi, how are you doing?" I greet a Linda.

"I'm fine. How are you?" Her movements are stiff.

"Are you on the Dream Team?"

"What?"

"A member of the Dream Team?" I say as I point to the sign explaining our membership system.

"Oh. Sorry, yes, I am." She shows me her card and says, "It's really busy today. Do you think this is because of what they said on the news?"

"I have been working all day. What did they say on the news?"

"Well, they said we might need to be prepared for a lockdown."

"Oh, *that's* what she was talking about."

"Huh?"

"Never mind. Damn. Really?"

"Yes. But no one gave any specific details on timing." Linda motions to her husband and asks, "Can you grab this?"

"Sure, babe." He looks at me and says, "What's going on, man?"

"Oh, nothing. Just talking about the apocalypse with your wife."

"Shit is scary, huh?"

"I guess. This is really the first I have heard of a *lockdown*. What does lockdown even mean?"

"They didn't say. But we want to be prepared."

I scan and judge their grocery selection. Some of the items make sense if you are going to be stuck at home—canned vegetables, canned tuna, pasta, sauce, rice, a vacuum-sealed meat selection—but a fair amount of the things they chose are perishable, such as veggies, banana cream pies, cookies, chips, four different types of coleslaw, fresh salmon, crab, and, of course, a healthy selection of our prepared foods. The cart is full of these items. I look back and see that everyone in my line has the same mounds of groceries. It seems excessive and gross.

They are not large people. They don't require this kind of consumption to maintain a lifestyle—at least from a physical standpoint. Most of the people in my line aren't overweight, and I doubt they have large families. They are hoarding. They are panicked, and now, suddenly, I am too.

"What do they want us to be prepared for?"

"The governor mentioned that schools might be closing soon."

"No shit?"

"Yeah, but they really left it at that. We left work early today to get some supplies."

I chuckle to myself a little as I ring up fresh caviar, fresh basil, fresh-pressed juices, fresh-fucking-everything. It's like they are preparing for a feast, not for a lockdown. How long can this food last? A week? Maybe two?

"How many kids do you have?"

"We have two boys. One is seven, and the other is nine," Linda responds.

The man's shoulders slump a little, and he says, "It's gonna be great fun."

Linda looks sideways at him, and his eyes veer away. "We will be fine," she retorts.

"Odds are we are going to be alright," I say to try to break the tension.

"Huh?"

"It's a Barenaked Ladies song," I say with a smile, but they are unimpressed. The conversation has turned south, and I am only about halfway through their groceries. I decide it's a good moment to focus on the work and sift through their purchases. They continue to argue as I ring up their items.

"You know, I think you need to be more positive about this whole thing," she pleads.

"I think *you* need to be more positive about this whole thing," he responds.

"Are you fucking mocking me? Are you a child?"

"Calm down. I'm just kidding."

"Well, I need you to be more positive. Especially in public. It makes us look like shitty parents if you act like the kids are a burden."

"Will it make you happy if I say they aren't?"

"Yes. And if you could just shut the fuck up."

I butt in. "Alright, your total is six hundred forty-nine dollars and thirty-two cents. Tips are nice but not mandatory."

Linda looks at me silently and puts her credit card in the reader.

"Have a great day."

"You too," she says.

As they walk away, I can hear the argument pick back up. I wonder what their home will look like for the next few weeks or months or however long this all drags on. But there is little time to wonder, because another cart filled to the brim with groceries awaits. I look back as far as I can, but I fail to see the end of the line. The endless parade of customers continues on throughout the morning as the tension builds and the shelves slowly empty.

The hysteria is blatant and loud and righteous as my well-to-do clientele shuffle into the checkout line like cattle at a slaughterhouse. Their faces are anxious and tight. And I don't see a smile for the entirety of my shift. I periodically hear shoddy translations of information from the governor through my customers like a poorly run game of telephone. Finally, my lunch break has arrived.

* * *

"Dude, what the fuck is going on down there? It's a madhouse," my excitable coworker and friend named Mary says as she sits down at the table next to me in the break room upstairs.

"I don't know. I am scanning through Twitter, and I'm getting a little worried."

"A little? I'm terrified."

"Yeah, everything is spinning out of control so fast. The internet is telling me that it's a conspiracy from the top levels."

"Really?"

"Yeah, but it's the internet. Take what you will from that dumpster fire."

"Can a few billion people be wrong?"

"Every. Fucking. Time, Mary. The bigger the group, the dumber the shit they believe."

"I see what you're saying, but this is a global pandemic. Spain, Japan, Australia—everyone is reacting in unison and taking it seriously."

"It's hard to think that we can understand what is going on. The smart people are lost. Everyone is conflicting with each other. We should take it seriously, though. I just don't know exactly what to take seriously."

"I know, right? I heard they're going to mandate masks."

"Yeah, I was just reading that."

"People are freaking out. I had a lady start crying in my line a little while ago."

"Wow. Really?"

"Yeah. I didn't know what to do. I just told her everything is gonna be alright and handed her the receipt. I didn't know what else to do. I wanted to give her a hug."

"You're so sweet, Mary. There isn't much else you can do, I guess," I assure her.

"You're right. I need to take a breath. My heart is full of dread, and I don't want to go back down there."

"Me neither."

"Everything is changing so quickly."

"Did you hear the governor sent kids home from school?" I ask.

"Like his own?"

I shake my head. "No, everyone's."

"Already? I heard it might happen, but there wasn't a confirmation."

"I read it on Twitter on the way up the stairs."

"This isn't going to go well."

"I know. I'm so worried. I feel like I'm spinning on a merry-go-round and no teacher is close to stop me from losing my shit."

"I guess we are the teachers?"

"I think you're on to something there, Mary," I say with a smile.

"Maybe my first duty as your teacher is to remind you that you got to the break room before me and my break is almost up."

"Shit! See you down there."

I run out the door as Mary begins to speak, clock back in, and jump down the stairs.

Mike isn't concerned with my ten-minute delay. In fact, everyone—even the supervisors—is too busy and preoccupied with managing the chaotic scene before them when I ask what register I should go to. Finally, after I've asked a few people for direction, someone says I need to go to register eight.

I hurry to my checkout stand after what seems like five minutes of walking past a riotous crowd of Lindas, Daves, Normans, Bryans, Chips, Todds, and Caitlyns—the weight of their uncertainty hits me harder than before. I spent the majority of my break perusing Twitter, half losing my mind, talking with Mary, growing increasingly terrified and paranoid. I did this to myself, but here I am.

* * *

Linda walks up to the cash register. She is wearing a mask. It's the first time I have seen someone in a mask. I am thinking that was impossibly quick, but here we are.

"Oh man . . . I guess I should get me one of those."

"I'm not taking any chances. I lived through the AIDS epidemic, you know."

"Interesting. That must have been a crazy time," I reply, and upon closer inspection, I notice she isn't wearing only a mask. She has gloves and trash bags wrapped around her wrists and ankles. She moves goggles to cover her eyes as she edges toward the credit card machine. They look like the kind welders wear.

"Yeah. It was scary as hell. No one knew what was gonna happen. You all need more protective equipment."

I want to remind her how the AIDS epidemic worked out and that maybe, just maybe, the hysteria wasn't warranted, but I think better.

"I'm more worried for all of you frontline folks, though. I mean, you are all out here, and a deadly virus has hit our shores. You are the real heroes in this."

"Heroes?"

"Yes. I mean, you are all putting your lives on the line here."

Cue the internal eye roll. I don't feel like I am putting my life on the line at all. But then again, I don't know anyone who has died from COVID-19. I don't really know much about the virus at all. "I don't know if I would call what we do *heroic*," I say.

"I would. Get used to it."

"I guess you are putting your foot down on this one, huh?"

"Yes sir. You don't get paid enough, either. Like, where is your personal protective equipment?"

"Honestly, this is literally the first day I am hearing about protective equipment, so I am not sure."

"You should talk to your boss about that."

"I'm sure something is in the works."

My general distrust of powerful people begins to simmer to the surface as she speaks to something I would consider true overall. No one cares about me or my coworkers. And it's a good thing. Accepting the loneliness of my circumstance helps me process any struggle in a meaningful way.

"I wouldn't be so sure."

"Why not?"

"Well, do they show that they care about you otherwise?"

"I guess not. But I don't think anyone is obligated to care about me. I don't really know where this conversation is going."

Ah, here is a fundamental disagreement. I don't need them to care. I don't need or want her to pass along this momentary consideration of my well-being as if she thinks about it normally. Is it fair to her for me to think she is lying? Probably not. And I wouldn't say she is being dishonest. But concern for others that is born out of fear is not as valuable to me as genuine, sustained empathy. Maybe she is telling the truth and she is deeply concerned about what happens in my world. I guess I will never know, but her position seems more patronizing than anything.

"Personal protective equipment."

"Okay. I will bring it up with my boss."

"Good. I am just so worried about you all."

I look back at the growing line, and my desire for this conversation to be over rises.

"What is your name?" she asks.

"Daniel."

"Well, David. I hope that you stay healthy and safe."

"Thanks, but my name is Daniel."

"Great. Well, have a good day."

"Ma'am, you still need to pay."

"Oh, sorry. Here," she says as she tries to hand me a credit card. I point to the credit card machine.

"Oh Lord, I am so sorry, David. I've lost my head today. This pandemic is really getting to me."

I saw the word *pandemic* on Twitter, but I don't really know what she means by it.

"No worries at all. Here is your receipt. You are all set."

"Well, thank you so much, David. Stay safe and healthy."

* * *

Norman steps into my line with a small basket of groceries.

Unprompted, he says, "I don't understand what the hubbub is all about. This thing is just like the flu."

"Umm . . . are you on the Dream Team?"

"God knows I'm not. That thing is a rip-off."

"It's free, sir."

"Well, I don't need the corporations tracking me."

Maybe he shouldn't shop at our store, then.

"I understand, sir. Did you bring—"

"And another thing. It shouldn't take so long to get through these lines of people. I waited twenty minutes. Such bullshit."

I skip the formalities and begin to ring up his groceries.

"Well, aren't you going to ask if I brought my own bags? I thought that was something that you people do here since this is one of those fancy fucking grocery stores."

"Do you have your own bags?"

"Of course not. Then I have to wash the bags. Double bag my groceries, though, why don't you."

"Sure. No problem."

"I can't believe they are thinking about shutting everything down. I've had tuberculosis twice, and I smoke cigarettes, and I'm not scared."

I look him over while I ring up the groceries. His gut protrudes over his dad jeans and peeks out from his T-shirt that claims, "I signed my death warrant in Mexico a long time ago. So you can kindly fuck off." What a lovely American.

"Have a great day," I say while handing him his receipt.

"This is such bullshit."

I turn away, hoping the next customer will hurry up so that I can greet them. Norman stands silently and waits for me to acknowledge him again.

"Did you need anything, sir?"

"I want to talk to your manager."

"Umm . . . okay," I say as I flip the switch to make the light above my checkout stand flash to signal for a manager.

"You are extremely fucking rude. You know that?"

I glance at him for a moment because I'm not sure if he is talking to me.

"Hey, asshole! I am talking to you!" he screams.

"I'm sorry, sir. I will call my manager over."

"Goddamn right you will."

No one is coming. I am beginning to panic. So I pick up the phone attached to my register.

Ring, ring. Ring, ring.

"Hey, what's up, Daniel?" Mike answers.

"I have a customer over here that is extremely upset and cussing at me. He is acting very irrational."

"I heard that, you little shit," Norman barks.

"Okay. I'll be right over."

My supervisor, Mike, arrives in less than a minute. I begin ringing up the next customer.

"Hello, sir. What seems to be the problem here?" Mike asks Norman.

"Well, this asshole is the problem." Norman jabs his finger in my direction.

"Excuse me, sir. There is no need for the language."

"I'm sorry. He just was so damn rude to me," Norman says as he backs off momentarily.

"Was it something he said?"

"No. It was more in his body language."

"His body language, sir?" Mike says with a hint of exasperation.

"Yeah. He acted like I was a problem from the moment I got in line. He was all tense and shit the whole time." Norman is undeterred.

"Well, if you look around real quick, you can see we are extremely busy, and I am sure he didn't mean anything by it."

"That may be, but I expect to be treated with respect when I shop here," Norman pleads.

"I understand, sir."

"Good. So do you have a gift card or something for me?"

"Sir?"

"A goddamn gift card for putting up with this shit!"

I see the exhaustion in Mike's eyes as he says, "Right this way."

A fat face with rosy cheeks pops up in front of me and sets down a jar of pesto. It's Linda, and she leans a little bit to make eye contact. I cringe as she says, "Don't worry about that asshole. Y'all are the real heroes here."

That is the second person in maybe ten minutes who has claimed that I am a hero. A sickness washes over me.

Immediately, she notices the unease in my face about the expression and begins slamming her other groceries on the conveyor belt. I hate feeling obligated to apologize. But that's customer service in a nutshell—you always have to do things you don't want to, and I hesitate momentarily to contemplate if I should save this conversation from going south. She means well.

"I'm sorry, ma'am. I didn't mean to cringe when you said that. I just don't know how to react to that particular compliment."

"It's fine. I was just trying to show my appreciation for you guys because I know how hard you have it," she says in earnest but continues to aggressively "place" items on the belt.

"Believe me. I understand."

"What does your name tag say? Daniel?" Her eyes begin to water. "I guess I'm scared, Daniel. I don't know what is going to happen next."

"These are definitely uncertain times."

"It all just happened so fast, ya know?"

"Yeah. Yesterday I had no idea that I'd be talking so candidly with a customer. Hell, I only started this job a few days ago."

"Oh my! I am sorry for dumping my stress on you. You are still learning everything."

"That I am."

"We all are. We are all in this together," she replies as her eyes shift down.

Despite how untrue her statement feels when I think about it, I reply, "Now more than ever."

I look behind her at the endless line of distraught patrons and think that these people need me more than I need them. My heart gives a half smile. I notice the end of my shift has come. I grab the phone at the register and dial 311 to reach a floor supervisor.

Ring, ring.

A customer shovels groceries onto the belt from a cart piled high.

Ring, ring.

I hold the phone aside to address the customer. "Hi, how are you?"

"Fine."

"Are you a Dream Team member?"

Ring, ring.

"No." He looks impatient. Fucking Dave and his shit.

The line behind him grows fragile and angry. I begin to scan groceries.

Beep. "How are you doing tonight?" Beep.

Ring, ring. "Yeah, I can't believe they are going to close schools. It's definitely scary out there."

Goddamnit. Why isn't anyone answering? Too many things going on at once.

Finally somebody answers the phone. "Hey, it's Daniel." Beep. "I'm scheduled to be off right now. Who is going to replace me?" Beep.

"Can you hold on for a little longer?" Beep. "Your replacement hasn't gotten here yet."

"Okay, will it be an issue if I go over my hours for the week?"

"I'm not gonna worry about it," the manager responds. Beep.

"How long do you think? Half hour?" The manager confirms. "Alright. Shit. Sorry about that, sir," I address the next customer. "What were you saying about the virus?" Beep. Beep. Beep. Beep. Beep.

* * *

It has been an hour since my call to the supervisor when the phone at my register rings. "Hey, dude," Mike greets me. "I know you are tired and you were about to go home, but do you think you can stay until close? We had a callout and could really use the help."

I contemplate my level of exhaustion and weigh it against the need for money. "Yeah, man. I can help. No problem."

"Okay. You are awesome. Also, there will be a guy coming through installing some plexiglass dividers here in a little bit. You can take a break then."

"Uh . . . dividers?"

"Yeah. Word came down from corporate that we need to start adding in dividers and providing additional personal protection equipment."

"A customer just mentioned something about PPE earlier. I guess this is serious, huh?"

"It seems so. We get updates periodically. I'll let you know what is happening when I find out."

"What time will he come by my register? I'm getting hungry."

"They should be at your register soon. Sorry, I don't have an exact time."

* * *

"Hi, sir, how's it going today?" I greet the next customer.

"Not sure, man. How are you?"

"I'm doing alright. The vibe has changed in here, though."

"I guess," he replies.

I gesture around me. "I mean, doesn't it feel more tense in here?"

"Yeah, it sure does. People are panic-stricken. The government is scaring them."

"The government is doing this?"

"Yeah, man. This virus doesn't kill most people. The elderly and people with pre-existing health concerns have to worry about it, but the rest of us will probably be fine."

"But what does that have to do with the government? Sounds like people are just worried in general."

"No, the government is the one giving only partial information, and the major media outlets are spreading that shit around. We need to live our lives and move on. We are all going to die one day."

"Yeah, but if that's preventable, shouldn't we try to avoid it?"

"Yes. But when this lockdown goes into effect, the economy will go to a near standstill. People are going to be out of work and desperate, and bad things are going to happen."

"And the government wants this to happen?" The earnestness I see in this man's eyes makes me want to believe him. I'm not much for authority, but it's stretching my imagination to think people would go to such lengths as to destroy society in order to gain power.

"Chaos breeds a desire for security. The government will step in, and even if what they do isn't successful, they will never relinquish that power they gained. This is a power grab and nothing more."

"So you don't think there is anything else to it?"

"As far as the taking of actual liberties? No. The virus is real, and it's bad, but that's not the end game here. This is a politician's wet dream. Those people long for power, and any opportunity to seize it will be taken. Politicians may start off from a well-intentioned place, but that's easily corrupted once they achieve the status and security that comes with the power. In their heart of hearts, they believe they can run your life better than you can, and through institutions composed of thousands and even millions of people, they are working towards the 'betterment of mankind.'"

"Wow. I didn't expect this deep of a conversation on a Saturday afternoon."

"Sorry, I'm a policy analyst at a think tank in Washington, DC, and it's my job to think about how public policy affects our lives. The virus has magnified the role of politicians and given credence for huge government overreach since late last year. I haven't had the opportunity to talk about it too much recently."

"By *policy analyst,* do you mean a regular on Reddit?" I ask, only half joking.

He laughs and says, "I guess we will never know."

"Well, you gave me plenty to think about."

"Good. I hope you have a great day."

"You too."

A man taps me on the shoulder. "Hi, I am here to install the plexiglass."

"Cool. Where is my replacement?"

"Not sure. They didn't say anything about that. Is it okay if I get started?"

"Yeah, that's fine. I still have to take the customers until they close me down."

"No problem. I'll stay out of your way."

"Is that possible with you putting up a glass shield between me and my customers?"

"Oh, good point. Do you want to call your boss?"

"Yeah. Hold on." I turn to a customer as he pushes his groceries up to the counter. "Sorry, sir. I might have to leave the station."

"Are you fucking serious, man?" he responds and continues to unload the groceries despite my warning.

"Sorry. We need to install some plexiglass."

He mutters something under his breath.

Ring . . . ring . . .

"Hi, this is Mike."

"Hey, Mike, the guy is here to install the plexiglass. I still have a line and can't work with him in this little space."

"For sure, man. Just go to break."

"I have a really big line. Not sure I can send them away without a full-scale riot."

"Oh, true. Okay. I'll be down in a second."

I see Mike walking over. He is wearing a mask and rubber gloves.

"Dude, are you going to check me out?" the impatient Dave from the line asks.

"I'm sorry, man," I answer. "I have to close down this lane. My boss is almost here. He will be able to check you out."

"What a poorly run operation."

"You're telling me."

Mike has arrived. "Hey, man . . . have a good break. Make sure you grab a mask and gloves when you go upstairs."

"Oh, okay," I say with a nervous chuckle.

* * *

The break room has expanded out into the hall. A few tables sit several feet away from each other, and a sign reading "Please Maintain Social Distancing Guidelines" looms above the chairs. The activity in the break room looks pretty normal, with people keeping mostly to themselves with their earbuds in and smartphones up to their faces. In the middle of the room is a table with personal protective equipment such as masks and gloves and face shields. I take some rubber gloves, a mask that reads "Hero"—I look around for another option instead of "Hero," but it looks like I am one whether I like it or not—and a face shield.

My robust beard begins to itch the moment I put on the mask. I can't stop. It feels like the weird time I had scabies. A sign says that the mask is required at all times and to remain six feet away from people. I look around the room, and everyone is wearing their gloves, masks, and face shields. They are spread out according to the six-feet guideline. I debate momentarily if I really care about the rules. I don't, because I'm young and healthy, but it is mandatory, and I need the money.

I take a seat in the corner of the room and begin to eat. As I ravage a burrito, I look up and see another employee staring at me with obvious judgement. He walks over to me and says something through his mask and face shield.

"What?" I ask. His voice is muffled, and I can't understand.

He speaks up again.

"Dude, I can't understand you."

He pulls his mask down and says, "I think you should probably eat that outside."

"Why would I do that?" I reply. I don't know this coworker, and I feel like he is intruding on my peace and quiet.

"Because you aren't wearing your mask."

"You want me to wear my mask while I'm eating? How would I do that?"

"You pull your mask down, take a bite, and then put it back up over your mouth."

I stare at him for a moment. "Yeah. I'm not doing that. I'm almost done anyway." I take a big bite of my burrito. He storms off.

Mary walks over and asks, "What happened there?"

"He asked me to eat outside because I'm not wearing a mask while I eat."

"Well, don't you think you should?"

"No, we are spread apart six feet, and he is wearing the face shield and mask. I think we will be okay."

"I heard that it can travel up to twenty feet," she replies. Despite the mask covering half her face, I can see her worry in the way her eyebrows knit together.

"Do you think the virus can travel through the ventilation system?" I ask her.

"Maybe."

"Well, then we should relax, because we are fucked either way. And by *we*, I mean he should chill out and let me eat my burrito."

"I get that. He is probably just scared like all of us."

"Believe me. I am too. But we have to function within reason, you know?"

"You're right. I am just letting the germaphobe inside take control here."

"Oh, who knows? Maybe I am underreacting. But I still think that guy can go fuck himself. I am not going outside in this shitty weather to appease his fears."

"Daniel. Relax. Now *you* are the one freaking out."

"I don't know where it's coming from," I say as I finish my burrito and put my PPE on.

"Can I sit down for a minute?" she asks.

"Of course."

Both of us are wearing our masks and face shields as we sit six feet apart at one of the round break room tables. I pull my mask out and scratch my face.

"How effective do you think the PPE is if it's wildly uncomfortable and I am constantly touching my face?" I ask.

"I'm sure it still mitigates the risk at least a little."

"Does it, though? It's not like I'm washing my hands all the time. Viruses spread on surfaces, like the flu."

"Good point. I really don't know the answer to that."

"What'd you say?"

She lowers her mask and says, "I don't know the right answer."

"See, you just touched your face again."

"Damnit, Daniel!"

We both laugh, and Mary asks, "Do you think it's okay that we are sitting so close?"

"Well, this is probably six feet, but I honestly have no idea what to think. We are dressed like brain surgeons more than grocery store cashiers. I get the feeling we will be alright."

"You're right. I'm being paranoid."

"Maybe you are, but it's hard not to be. Every time I look at the news or go online, some new guideline is up. It's almost as if they are making us paranoid on purpose."

"Who?"

"The people in power."

"You think so?"

"Well, I had a conversation with a customer earlier, and he's got my mind churning. But, really, I don't have a clue. I just know that's what it feels like."

"So I am not alone."

"Nope. I'm right there with you. And here we are on the front lines of it all. Do you think we will get a raise?"

She shrugs. "I sure hope so. People have been calling me a hero all day. I think we deserve some hero pay."

"I agree. Hopefully they will do something for us."

"It's miserable down there. Every customer is a new weight on my chest."

"Just remember that you are a hero," I say.

We both laugh. I realize I'm five minutes over on my break. "I need to go."

"Okay. I'll see you down there."

* * *

We are near closing time when I reach the front end and check in with our manager. But it doesn't feel like the end of anything. Every cashier looks cornered, with hollow stares and labored faux niceness.

"Can you head to express?" Mike asks me.

"Yeah, no problem. Are we going to close on time tonight?"

"We are going to close as soon as possible," he responds with an anguished look.

"Alright. Sounds good," I say, but he doesn't respond. "Hey, man, what's wrong?"

"It's nothing."

"Nah, dude. What's up?" I push.

"I read an article that said they expect up to *four* million deaths from the virus no matter what we do."

"Woah. I saw a clip saying it was two million. Four is a crazy amount. Are you sure?"

He nods. "Yup. Experts are saying it."

"Well, the clip I read about two million dead was from experts too. Maybe they are both wrong."

"Could be. But look at all of this shit. It's madness."

"Mike, come here." I put my arm around his shoulders.

"This isn't exactly social distancing, Daniel."

"That's okay. See, because you're a hero, Mike."

He laughs.

"Heroes don't get the virus."

"Are you sure?" he asks.

"I've never been so right."

"Good. And thanks, man. I needed that."

Right now, the express lane is busier by sheer volume of customers compared to the bigger registers because it caters to people who aren't hoarding their groceries or already have the essentials and just need some small items. But it also brings in the stragglers, fiends, and drug addicts as the night wears on. I am familiar with this lifestyle, because from time to time, I am one of them. I haven't ever drunkenly shopped at Dream Grocers, though. I usually reserve shenanigans for my local marketplace, where I can afford to go grocery shopping. There are many times in my life when I have asked an Uber to stop at a supermarket, after visiting my local bar, so I can get late-night snacks. Dream Grocers wasn't justifiable until I started working here.

We receive a discount, but it's only enough to make shopping affordable sometimes, because with this job I also took a huge pay cut, so really, it's a wash. My mouth waters at the decadent foods that go through my register, but I understand the place I am at in life. This is the in-between times—or so I'd like to think. But I have noticed a certain cross section of young people who come through my line. They are the type who don't look at their credit card statements. There are no second thoughts as they put the card in the machine. It's not a judgement; it's the reality of who comes through. Even as a pandemic rages on, they don't seem concerned.

Three younger adults with hollowed-out eyes, colorful masks, and dilated pupils walk into my line. I overhear their conversation while I check out another Linda.

"There isn't anything to do anymore," one of the young adults says.

"What?"

"I said there isn't anything to do."

"We are doing something right now."

"I mean besides drugs and Dream Grocers."

"I think you need to be more positive. Me and Abby are having a great time."

"We are?" the girl—who I assume is Abby—replies.

"Of course we are. We all have unemployment, and we don't really need it. This pandemic is going to be great."

"I don't know. Honestly, I feel kind of bad about taking unemployment," she says, and all three laugh.

Before they set anything on the conveyor belt, the tallest boy walks up to my register. He asks, "Hey, man, so I noticed you all don't have some sandwich wraps out on the shelf over there." He points to the general area of prepared foods. "Do you think you can have them whip something up for me really quick?"

"I'm part of a different department, but I know they don't do one-offs. They make things in mass production, not like a restaurant."

He stares at me with his sunken eyes perched over his mask that says "Fuck Capitalism."

After a moment, he responds, "Listen, man—I'm not trying to be a pain in the ass, but I'm really hungry, and I could use something to eat."

I want to hold out my hand like Willy Wonka and make this young man see the wonderment that is Dream Grocers and all of the edible delights available to him, but I say, "Yeah, sorry, man. If we don't have the item on the shelf, it's not available."

"They did it for me last time."

"Well, did you ask anyone in that department if they have some available?"

"Look, bro, I'm asking nicely. I don't think we need to talk to your manager, do we?"

"Here, I'll call him."

Ring, ring, ring . . . "Hey, Mike, a customer would like to talk to you."

The customer shakes his head. "I said that I don't want to talk to a manager. I just want you to see if they can whip up a sandwich for me."

"Sir, they don't make individual sandwiches," I respond dryly.

"They have before, and they will again." He is furious now. I wave to his friends to come up, but the angry guy places his stuff on the conveyor belt and says, "I got this."

Over the loudspeaker, a voice says, "Attention, Dream Grocers team members and guests, we will be closing in ten minutes."

Mike arrives. "What seems to be the problem?"

"This gentleman would like a sandwich wrap we don't have on the shelf."

"Hi, sir, did you talk to our prepared-foods department?" Mike addresses the angry man.

"About what?" the customer asks, dumbfounded.

"About the sandwich you would like," Mike responds.

"Nah, man. We got everything we need right here." The customer does a one-eighty in tone and demeanor.

"So you didn't have a question about our sandwiches?"

"Yeah. I'm not sure what this guy is talking about."

"Wait, what?" I say as my agitation with this asshole grows.

"Yeah, man. I think you misunderstood me. We just need these items."

Mike looks at me and says, "Okay. Well, let me know if you need anything else."

The loudspeaker crackles again. "Attention, Dream Grocers team members and guests, we will be closing in five minutes."

As Mike steps away, the customer leans toward me. "Yo. That wasn't cool. I was just trying to deal with you one on one, and you brought your manager over here. I mean, we're good with this stuff, but I expect to be treated better next time."

"Huh?"

"Did I stutter? Ring up my shit."

I contemplate fracturing his skull. "Receipt is in the bag."

"Make my sandwich next time, bitch," he says and starts to walk away.

"Don't come in the store high on drugs next time, bitch."

He turns around. "What the fuck did you say to me?"

I pull down my mask a little and say, "I said don't forget your bag and your sandwich." I point at his wrap on the counter.

"Oh, thanks."

Mike walks up to my register. "You can shut down for the night, man."

"Okay. Thanks."

"What happened with that last customer? It felt like a glitch."

"Yeah, man. I don't know, but he definitely wanted that sandwich, then changed his personality when you came over, then reverted back again after. The thing was that he had a sandwich the whole time."

"Things are getting strange."

"I've been told it's the Fever Dream Grocers."
"True. Okay. Well, get out of here."

* * *

It's late when I arrive home, and my neighbors aren't on the patio. It will be a while before I can fall asleep. There is too much to process, and I'm wired.

I pull out a camping chair and sit in the doorway of my apartment. I throw on a pair of sweats and house slippers and wrap myself in a blanket. It's cold enough outside to see my breath, but I don't particularly care. I'm exhausted from the day but curious about what others are doing in their lives. What will my neighbors say?

I sit quietly in hopes that I'll hear the world shift. Tiny portals of light flicker across my view from the doorway. I wonder if the people inside those windows feel trapped or hopeless like the Lindas and Daves I've met this week. The only sound I hear is of a helicopter off in the distance.

In a tall brown building across the courtyard, a woman is standing at her sink washing dishes. A man comes up behind her and puts his hands around her waist and kisses her neck. She leans back, revealing that she is pregnant. They whisper only inches from each other; then he gets on his knees and places his ear on her belly and talks.

I wonder what kind of world that child will grow up to rebel against his or her parents in. It's a pandemic, for Christ's sake. This is the real deal. When he or she is born, will the mother's face be covered by a mask? My generation is already becoming detached from reality.

We are going to birth an entire generation afraid of an invisible monster and the political force behind it. This is how slaves are made.

I realize now that I'm spiraling out inside of my own head. That's not good. I need to remain grounded and in control. I work tomorrow. I'll be in the pit again, facing more Lindas and Daves in my essential role.

The lights dim in the pregnant couple's house. A pandemic almost seems like the perfect time to procreate. Right now, it is wise to keep your life focused on something as singular and important as taking care of your offspring.

In a different window, I see a family sitting in front of a TV, with two young boys wrestling around. I hear muffled yelling coming from that general direction. Their fighting begins to escalate. Fists start to fly. One boy's legs whirls upward into the TV, knocking it away from the wall, and it turns off. The yelling is louder now. A man from the other room rushes in and grabs one boy and pulls him away from the violence. He is red faced as he holds one by the shirt collar and proceeds to scream. The child is kicking and fighting the man holding him. He manages to knock over the lamp, and the scene goes dark.

What just happened? Was that our future?

In the apartment below, I can see a couple—probably in their late twenties—sitting at a kitchen table looking over some papers. The conversation seems serious. If I were a betting man, I would say they are looking at bills and making hard decisions—wondering what luxuries to cut from their budget. Will Netflix have to go, or will it be not ordering takeout anymore? Either way, their lifestyle is changing. Unexpected sacrifices will be made. At first, they will make the easier ones, but soon it will get more difficult. Maybe they will have to move back into their parents' house. And he promised her the life she'd always dreamed of. Will their love survive?

And to think this shit has only just begun. That's a hard fucking truth that we will all have to deal with—both essential and non—whatever those terms really mean. I decide it's best to call it a night and head into my dark, lonely apartment. At least I know there are others out there in the madness trying to understand or get through what I know we should.

Chapter Five

The breaking light of the day stretches through the window as I pour a cup of coffee out of the French press, then walk out onto my balcony. It's so quiet I can almost hear the steam rise from my cup. The normally busy streets are lifeless.

Jason is smoking a cigarette on the patio.

"Man, it's so quiet out here," he says between drags.

"Right? Except for the helicopters."

"Yeah, I noticed that. I don't see them flying by, but I hear them all of the time now. Is that because no one is driving? Were they always flying overhead?"

"I'm not sure. I just know that it's getting old."

"When do you go to work?" he asks.

"At seven a.m. I have a feeling it's going to be a long day. And why the hell are you up so early?"

"Couldn't sleep. My work told me that they will be putting me on furlough until further notice."

"For real? Why?" I ask.

"They said the government is going to announce something big tomorrow. Tonight we'll drink whiskey."

"I think that's a great idea," I reply and ask, "What are you going to do to pay rent?"

"I have some savings, and I'll file for unemployment."

"Seems reasonable."

"It's the only option at the moment," Jason responds with a shrug.

"That's fair. Well, I have to get going. So I'll catch you tonight for some whiskey drinking? We can listen to the neighbors too."

"I heard someone talking when I came outside."

"What were they saying?" I ask.

"It was some dude on a patio, talking on his phone, saying this whole thing is a hoax. Hold on. Let's see if we can still hear him."

The man's voice is distinct as he preaches into his phone: "Yeah, man, the president says it's not that big of a deal. Well, yeah, I know that he might not know what he is talking about, but he would have a lot more information than we would. Ah, yeah, that's true. He isn't an epidemiologist. I mean, honestly, I'm looking at the symptoms, and I think I had this shit back in January. Yeah, I know it could've been a cold. You think you had it too?"

My coffee is warm in my hand as I relax on the sun-drenched patio in the heart of the deathly quiet city watching a front of troubling weather roll over the mountains. The man's conversation goes on like this for quite some time. The volume of his voice waxes and wanes. It's as if he is trying to convince himself of some noble truth. The sounds of helicopter blades drown out the man and his pleas.

"I'm telling you, dude," the man says in earnest. "They are going to gain so much power from this whole thing. It has to be a power grab." The conversation seems to end just as the helicopter noise fades away.

It's quiet for a few moments; then Jason exclaims, "Damnit! I wanted to hear more."

"What do you think?" I ask him.

"About what?"

"About the power-grab comment at the end."

"Oh yeah. Of course this will be a power and cash grab for some people. But that doesn't mean I think it is a hoax."

"That's true. People are getting sick. And the government always gains power from these moments in history."

"And it's only just begun."

* * *

The front end of the store looks trampled. The atmosphere inside the store is solemn, and the shelves are beginning to look scarce. The night crew can't keep up with the demand of the customers. Backstock on almost every item is dwindling down to scraps. Essential items are all but ghosts on the shelf. We don't carry much toilet paper, but it's completely gone except the little bit that management stored upstairs in the office. I will have to seek out one of them if I'm in need. Luckily, I have plenty of toilet paper at home, and I think I'll be able to make it a few weeks.

I find myself asking, Why in god's name would people stock up on paper towels and toilet paper for an end-of-the-world scenario? I can think of numerous items that one might consider when locking down for a long haul. Maybe the irrational fear of being stuck at home for months with martial law in effect gripped them in the middle of the night; then visions of toilet-paper-bartering hordes roaming across the apocalyptic world forced them to buy as much as they could manage.

Fear makes people do strange things. On my way to work, a woman traveled across the street to avoid walking by me. Once I passed, she moved back to my side of the street. It's going to take a long time for her to get anywhere if she is living in the city and trying to avoid people.

I don't know how deadly the virus will be, but I am sure that living as if people are constant threats will not help anyone's mental health. But she wasn't the only one. I saw folks cowering in fear everywhere as I walked toward arguably the most dangerous place you could be going during a pandemic, with the exception of a hospital.

I don't want to be like that, and frankly, I don't have a choice. Nothing positive will come from living in fear for me. Live and let live, so they say. It's still scary not knowing which Lindas and Daves will have the virus. And I need to pay my bills. My choice has been made for me by circumstance, but like I said earlier, I did this to myself. That must be where I hold my ground mentally and resolve to make it through.

Upstairs, by the time clock, employees are gathered around the whiteboard. A message reads:

Hi All,

I know everyone has questions for store leadership. We don't have a ton of answers at the moment because we are still waiting for information from Federal and State authorities, but this is the information we have so far.

We are approving all overtime right now. If you want to work more hours please talk to your management.

Corporate has approved a $3 raise for all employees effective immediately. This will be reflected on your next paycheck.

Our attendance policy will be put on hold for the time being. These are stressful times and we do not want you to feel burdened to come in under duress. Please direct any questions to your supervisor.

Several work environment related announcements:

We have PPE such as masks available for you in the break room.

Please maintain the proper social distance as much as possible. We will be rearranging some of our areas to accommodate the new guidelines.

We will also be changing the layout of the store in some areas for your safety. Plexiglass between you and the customers and so on.

If you are struggling in any way please reach out to your supervisor. We are a team here at Dream Grocers.

"Well, hell yeah to more money," one employee says.

"Why am I hearing about all of this for the first time?" I ask. "I already have all my PPE, and they put up the plexiglass yesterday."

"Yeah, dude, it seems like we are all playing catch-up with this thing."

"Well, but are we being protected?"

"Of course not, but I need the money."

"That's fair. I don't have another option at the moment either," I respond as I realize I'm going to be late if I don't clock in within the next five minutes. I run to the coatrack, put my backpack away, and race over to sign in.

A tense early-morning crowd is waiting for the front door to open. In my short tenure at the store, never have I witnessed such a motley crew of Lindas and Daves crouched, ready to pounce on organic produce and ethically raised free-range chicken breasts. Elderly folks are usually the ones waiting to enter the store in the dawn's early light. They have been up for hours and have no concern for those of us who do not get up early on a regular basis. That is not the case this morning. No, today, a horde of all ages is waiting to pillage the sanctum of the Grocery Cathedral.

I slowly sip on my first cup of coffee while people ransack the store. All I want is for them to take their time pillaging the freshly stocked shelves, but a line begins to form quickly, and my moment of solace vanishes as a customer walks up to my register. She is friendly and polite. But I realize that I can't understand what she is saying to me. Everything is muffled. And my voice sounds louder because the sound bounces right back to me. Luckily, she has only a few items. We exchange pleasantries and go through the motions.

As I attempt to chat with her, I notice that a line of maybe ten or twelve people is building at my register. I look over at the other opening cashier, and her line is empty. The customers aren't seeing the opportunity to leave faster, because I am on the main register. With the best of intentions to get the next customers out of the store faster, I lean over and say, "Hey, the register is open down there."

Dave is standing next to his wife, Linda. I can see how this is gonna go. His arm goes straight out with an open hand facing up, and he says, "What the fuck is wrong with this line?"

"Nothing is wrong with it. The other one is wide open," I respond.

He pauses momentarily, looks down toward the other register, and storms off.

I look back at the woman I am ringing up. We both shrug. "I guess some people . . ." she says, but I don't catch it all.

"What's that?" I yell.

"I said . . . some people didn't handle the news well."

"What news is that?" I ask.

"Oh, you know, the virus news."

"Ah, yes. Scary stuff," I say with a sigh.

"I guess."

"You're not worried?"

"No, I'm not hurried. Take your time."

"No. Not hurried. Worried!"

"Oh, yeah, no not really. I was reading that it's just like a flu."

"Really? I was reading that it's extremely contagious."

"So is the flu."

"That's fair. I guess I just don't know enough," I admit.

"Neither do I. I'm just not going to worry about it right now. I have a large stockpile of food at the house anyway."

"Ah, I see. Well, would you like your receipt in the bag?"

She gives me a strange look, then says, "What?" Then she waves her hand, saying, "Sure. Whatever."

"Have a great day, and be safe."

Once she walks away, I see Christian across the aisle. We both nod in a sleep-deprived early-morning sort of way. He points behind me. I look over and see what resembles a crowd at a professional football game rushing the doorway. I turn back around. Christian is busy with a new customer. Another Linda is loading my register's belt with items. I have no time to think. So I just react.

"Hi, how are you doing?" I ask.

"Oh hell, I don't know. How are you doing?"

"I'm alright. It's a busy morning."

"I can see that. Did you hear what the governor said?"

"No. What did he say?"

"We are all going to die."

"Wait . . . what did you say?" I respond. Surely he wouldn't have said such a thing.

"All we can do is try. Like try to live. Ya know?"

"Ah, yes. Now I know what you mean."

"What did you think I said?"

"I thought you said the governor said that we are all going to die."

She pauses for a moment, then says, "Do you really think he thinks that?"

"No. I don't think so. I mean, he didn't actually say that. I thought you did."

"Well, alright," she replies in a pensive tone.

* * *

I've manned the cattle chute for a few hours, and it's time for my break. Mike walks by, and I wave him down.

"Hey, dude. It's time for my break."

"Oh, damn. Okay. Hold tight, and we will figure it out."

I look back at the customer in front of me, who says, "The managers here always look worn thin."

"Yeah, they have a lot on their plates but take it on like a champ. Mike is a good dude," I respond.

"You should all get paid more for this shit."

"I agree. I think they will do something for us."

The customer waves off my comment. "Those greedy bastards don't care about you guys."

"Well, I don't know if that's—"

"Don't you see the news? They are making you all use PTO for the coronavirus."

"Well, that's not—"

"I can't believe they let the heroes go on starving during a pandemic," he responds before I can answer.

I'm losing patience with the one-way conversation. "I wouldn't say we are starving by any means."

"Can you live off of the money you make?"

"I'm getting by, but this isn't a forever job for me."

"What about the person who has invested ten-plus years in this place?"

"I'm not sure what you want me to say here."

"I want you to realize you are getting screwed."

"Do you? Or do you want me to know that you are aware that I'm getting screwed? I know how much I get paid."

"If you don't get it, then I don't know if I can help you."

"Sir, I am not sure if you are trying to help me. Here is your receipt."

This Norman is in over his head. He hasn't thought through the whole scenario, including what a cashier might think about their own circumstance. But that doesn't matter. He has made up his mind and placed me strictly as some sort of victim in his mind. Either way one might land on that issue, it does not help that he lectures me.

"Thank you. I hope you think about the price you are paying," he says as he drops a twenty-dollar bill onto the conveyor belt and walks away.

I grab the cash and stuff it in my pocket before I think anyone notices. We aren't allowed to take money from customers. I glance down at the end of the register, and Mike is looking at me. I feel a sense of shame wash over me, but that quickly evaporates. Maybe that Norman was right? I'm not paid much for my work, and apparently my job became much more dangerous. It is still my choice to be here. So I stand by my original thoughts, and I am taking his money because I need it. Nothing more, nothing less.

"Are you ready for a break?" Mike asks.

"Yes sir."

"Good. See you soon," he says as I walk past him.

I don't know what to do with the tip, because I feel like I hardly deserve it. I'm surprised that Mike didn't say something.

As I am walking upstairs, I notice the cash-office door is open halfway. Inside, I see a woman with tears running down her face and a supervisor talking to her. I walk past the door and stop to listen to see what is wrong. "I just can't handle this bullshit," the young woman exclaims.

"What happened?" another voice asks—the supervisor, I assume.

"It's not one specific thing. It's everything. And that I have to be here."

"Everything? What do you mean?"

"All the customers are being assholes while calling us heroes. They dump their baggage on us as if we aren't affected by the virus. I'm not paid enough for this. I'm not a therapist. They get to go home. I still have to be here."

"This is a tough time for everyone. Do you need to go home?"

"I do. I really do. But I won't get paid for it."

"I wish we could, but it's not our call."

"I know. Can I just go outside for a bit?"

"Of course."

I walk away. I *feel* her pain. I have been thinking the same thing all fucking day. And now I have only eight minutes until I need to go back down to the torrent of ugliness below.

I sit at one of the tables in the hall and peel off my mask and shield and lie open to the world. A rush of oxygen comes in, and my body feels warm. My eyelids are heavy, and my vision begins to fail. I lay my head down on the table.

Someone shakes me as I come to and lift up my head. "You alright, man?" It's Neal, the coworker with a straightforward nature and constant one-liners voice.

"Huh, yeah, I must have passed out."

"Yeah. I saw you fall asleep so hard your head bounced off the table. You okay?"

"I think so. I felt a rush of blood and then went out like a light."

"Was it the mask?"

"I don't think masks do that to people. Maybe it was the pressure," I admit.

"Yeah, this place has the compression and sound of a teakettle."

"It feels empty, too, oddly enough. Oh, and the lingering tension that hangs with every customer's response."

"Does it feel like you're treading water and wearing a sweat-ringed, rented weight vest to you also?"

"And I am holding up a locally sourced quiche in one hand and swiping their Visa Black in the other."

He chuckles. "We keep using all of these fantastic metaphors."

"How about we are slowly suffocating in the nauseous anxiety of strangers?" I say.

"Apt."

"Thank you."

"How shall we overcome?" Neal responds.

"Hold my hand." I extend my arm.

"Why?"

"Just do it. Now take a deep breath," I instruct.

"Okay. What next?"

"Hold on. Take another breath. Now imagine finding that last bag of pasta some Linda is searching for downstairs."

"Okay. I found it."

"Now dump it out on the floor."

He tilts his head. "Wait, why?"

"Just do it."

"But someone needs the food."

"Who cares? It's your dream. Have fun with it."

"Dream?"

"Duh."

* * *

I hear a knock on the door from my pitch-black bedroom. It's my neighbor Jason with a bottle of whiskey in his hand.

"What's up, man? You didn't forget about drinking, did you?"

"I completely forgot about it," I confess, "but I'm still down."

"I can imagine. How was work?"

"Long and terrifying."

"I was watching some news coverage of the stores. It's crazy."

"To say the least. I'm so exhausted. So what do you all think about this craziness?" I ask him, relieved to have a normal conversation.

"I'm kinda worried, man. I applied for unemployment, but the system is so backlogged that I don't know when it will come in," Jason replies.

"Damn, dude. Do you have savings?"

"I do, but who knows how long this will last?" he says before passing a shot of bourbon. "It feels like a trap, you know? Being forced out of work and into the arms of the government."

"Yeah, it's definitely going to add stress to everyone's lives. I wish I had some answers. But I'll take some shots with you."

Talking to Jason about his situation brings me back to the customer concerned with the government overreach and a power grab. I feel for Jason. He is a good man, and I wonder what will happen to him.

"Some of the neighbors are going down to the patio. Let's do this."

I grab some glasses, and we head down to our community patio. Levy and his girlfriend, Donna, are already there when we arrive. Levy waves at us to come quickly. We sit down.

"Dude, we can hear the neighbors," he says.

"Which neighbors?" Jason asks.

"Not sure. It's so fucking quiet out that I think their voices are bouncing off the courtyard walls."

A joint is passed around, and we begin to pour and puff our anxieties away.

"Anything interesting happening?" I ask.

"Not yet . . . shh . . . I think I hear something."

The whiskey ignites my throat. I hear a faint voice echoing off the courtyard walls and say, "I can barely hear . . ."

"Shh . . . it's the guy who was yelling from before. If you listen closely, you can hear it."

I swallow my whiskey and focus.

More clearly now I hear a woman shout, "You fucking idiot!"

"Oh man," I say softly.

"Goddamnit, what do you want?" a man replies.

"I want you to listen to me."

"We are stuck in this fucking house together. Listening to you is all there is to do."

"It's all the time. It's not just . . ."

The voice trails off. We wait a moment to talk. "Woah, that's crazy," I say.

"I know, right?" Levy responds. "Before you two got out here, we were listening to these two people lose their shit. From what we can gather, they are fighting about what to stream on Netflix. But there are a few conversations going on."

"Seriously?" I ask.

"Yeah, man. The voices are clear as day with no road noise, although those damn helicopters keep flying overhead."

"It's so annoying, and I can't see them," Jason says, almost as if he is talking to himself.

"They hide in the clouds," Levy responds, and we all laugh. Levy leans over and says, "That dude we just listened to called her a cunt. And then she yelled about how she is cheating on him. It's fuckin' bananas."

"Wow. Do you think they are having makeup sex now?" I inquire in hopes that they are, just for entertainment's sake.

"I would say it's a good possibility. Stupid arguments like that should always end in sex," Jason says. "I wonder how many couples are doing that right now?"

"Having makeup sex?" Levy says and cackles.

"Well, yeah, but also arguing over stupid shit. I am sure there is an epidemic of dumb arguments going on when people have to spend every waking moment with people they usually only see a few hours a day," Jason says.

"Yeah. No kidding," Levy says and looks off into the distance.

"What are the other conversations going on?" I ask.

We force a laugh for no particular reason, maybe because we are stoned, that echoes out into the court-yard on the cold March night. Is it actually spring? I forget. This is a time when what looks dead reveals itself alive. Flowers, trees, and animals are supposed to erupt back out into the world. Not the opposite.

A voice inside my head says, *But death is coming, like that strange Linda said at the store.* It sounds profound to me at first, but it's not. And that's okay. The warm embrace of whiskey masks any true feelings or fears. Our conversation floats on to all matters of the time. And this year is turning into a dumpster fire before our eyes. I envision drunken nights like this for the foreseeable future as we try to escape the world outside and in. Tragedy is coming for many folks, and I hope we are not the ones who fall in its path.

Chapter Six

I'm rattled awake by the ringing of my phone. My hangover anxiety is palpable as I answer. "Hello?"

"Hey, Daniel, it's Mike. How are you doing today?"

"I'm doing alright. Just waking up."

"Wanna make some extra money?"

"Sure. What time are you thinking?"

"Oh, as soon as you can get here."

"Okay. Give me a little bit. I have to ride my bike to work."

"Oh, that's right. Okay. Well, see you as soon as you can get here."

"Sounds good."

I hold my phone back to focus on the clock. It's six o'clock. Goddamnit! It's so early. I want to cry.

I dry heave over the toilet for a few moments, begging for anything to come out, but nothing does. I need the money, and capitalism never sleeps. The voice in my head chastises me at the prospect of working today, but I did this to myself. I don't have any plans for my day off, only rest. Instead of a beautiful day dedicated to recovery and Netflix, I try a short meditation on the couch, become frustrated, and then start getting ready for work.

I have numerous missed calls, text messages, and Facebook chats from my friends and family asking if I am okay. I feel out of the loop, so I look online to see if there are any updates. The governor has declared that Colorado is in a state of emergency. The news rattles me a bit, but I need to get going. I respond to as many people as I can, jump in a cold shower, brush my teeth, dry heave some more, and head out the door.

On my bike ride to work, I notice the streets are unusually empty and free for movement, so I turn west on Sixth Avenue and go against the grain. I'm nervous at first, as I expect to see headlights at any moment on the normally busy street. My legs churn. My heart thumps in my chest. Thump thump. Five blocks go by. Thump thump. Seven blocks. Thump thump. As I pass the eighth block, car lights appear over the hill. I swerve to the right down an unfamiliar street steeped in darkness to avoid being hit by a car. Sweat dampens my clothes. But my pulse subsides as I look at the homes filled with people who lie dormant like the trees.

I pull into the grocery store's parking lot and walk up to the normal entrance doors. They won't open. I see Mike inside, and he points to the second door farther down the building.

He opens the normally automatic door by hand. "What's going on?" I ask.

"Sorry, man. I should have told you. We have some new procedures going on."

"Like what?"

"Well, we have to take the temperature of every employee every time they go in and out of the place."

"What? Really? Even on lunch and fifteen-minute breaks?"

"Yup."

"Shit. What else?"

"Well, you have to sign in. So do that real quick. We have custom masks for everyone to wear. Take this one."

I look at the mask. It reads "Living the Dream." I look at Mike.

"I know it's corny, but I just do what I am told." He holds up his hands in self-defense. "Come over here so I can put this temperature gun up to your head."

"Uh, okay. This has to be quite a morose scene to see. What's my temp?"

"Ninety-six point eight."

"Well, that's probably not good. Isn't my body temperature supposed to be ninety-eight point six or something?"

"Yeah, but you are fine. There is an acceptable range."

"What's the range?"

"Just don't let anyone be over one hundred point two. Anything higher is considered a fever."

"That's it?"

"Yup, that's it. Do you think you can handle managing this thing?"

"What do I do if they are over temperature?"

"Oh yeah, well, ask them to stay outside, and then call for management."

"Okay. Sure. But wait, that's why you called me in?"

"Yeah. I couldn't tell you this morning. They want to keep everything hush hush. It's dumb, I know. But it seems like they are making everything up as they go."

"That's for sure."

"They are going to have a limit on the amount of customers allowed in the store too. So we might switch you to the front door at some point. We will have a cart person and a door counter up front."

"Jesus."

"Yeah, man. Shit is crazy. Go clock in, and we will get you situated."

"Okay."

As I pass the whiteboard near the time clock, there is another long list of updates on procedures that are going into effect, but I'm in a rush to get downstairs and get to work. I contemplate stopping to read everything, but I'll just learn as I go.

A new shift of employees is shuffling in as I get down to my post at the temperature check.

"Heyo!" I greet them. "Just write your name on the paper right there, and then I'll take your temperature."

"Is this really necessary?" one employee asks.

"I guess so. All the information you will need is upstairs near the time clock."

"This is goddamn ridiculous."

"Alright, my man, here is your mask . . . and you do not have a fever. Have a great shift."

Next a friendly and slightly stoned face appears in front of me.

"Hey, Christian. Welcome to paradise!"

"What is this shit?"

"It's a cavity scan. You ready?"

"I was born ready."

"Okay. Good. Now can you please write down your name and then come over so I can check your temperature?"

"Sure."

A moment later, I hold the temperature gun to his forehead. "Great. You passed. Did you see that fresh hell waiting at the front door?"

"Yeah, man. It's a huge line."

"Lindas, Daves, and Armageddon."

"No kidding. Did you hear that the virus might be airborne?"

"Is Ebola airborne?"

"Who knows?"

I shrug. "Google might know, but I gotta do this shit. Here, man. I'll talk to you later. Oh, wait. Here is your mask."

"Cool. Wait, what in the fuck . . ."

"Yeah, I know. Not the greatest phrase to put on the mask, huh?"

"Yeah. But I guess nightmares are dreams too."

"Ain't that the truth. I'll talk to you later."

Beautiful Lila walks through the door. Her rosy smile and long hair brightens anyone's day.

"Hey, Lila! How are you?"

"Well, I don't know, really," she admits.

"Me neither. I'll just take it day by day.'"

"That's all we can do."

"And wash your hands."

"Ah, good point. Everyone should've been doing that anyway."

"So true. Have a good shift. Here is your mask."

"Living the dream? My god, that's awful."

"It's someone's dream, for sure."

"True. I'll be your dream, Daniel," she flirts lightheartedly.

I blush. "You already are, Lila."

She blows a kiss and walks away. I think to myself that she's the girl I want to marry.

She makes me excited to work in this place.

* * *

Virtual shoppers and normal employees pour in and out of the store, and every one of them looks confused and irritated. Just moments ago, a virtual shopper barked, "Why the fuck do I have to do this shit?" when I asked him to stop so I could check his temperature with the gun.

All I could say was, "It's not my call."

He shrugged and said, "Seems pretty invasive to me."

I didn't know what to say in response, but I kinda wished it was a real gun in my hand when he pushed back against me doing my job. That'd change his tune quickly. And he might refrain from making his personal problems mine.

The job of watching the employee entrance has taken a dark turn. I am starting to hate the people, the situation, the whole fucking thing.

Christian is walking by to take his break. He stops. "You okay, man? Your face looks hollow."

"I hate it here, man. Everyone is in a shit mood with terrible things to say. It started out fine. Now, I don't want to be here anymore."

"I get that. People are taking their frustrations out on you. Just remember you are the gatekeeper. Hell, we all hold the key here at Dream Grocers. This is where your dreams come true."

I want to laugh but can muster only a smile. "That's a good point."

"I say don't let them in if they fuck with you."

"Do you think the store would back me up?"

"Oh god no! This 'dream' they sell at this market is more like a nightmare," he says with a laugh.

"You are not the first person to say that to me today."

"It's true."

"Sure feels like it. Hey, if you see Mike up front, can you tell him I need a break?"

"Sure thing."

A few moments later, Mike arrives. "Break time, eh?"

"Yes sir."

"Okay. I'll watch the door. When you get back, I am going to switch you to the front door, alright?"

"Whatever you say, boss."

"Great. Have a good break."

* * *

My stomach is rumbling. Everything is closed down in our prepared-foods department, so I look for a frozen burrito to hold me over until lunch. Two Lindas are in a heated discussion with each other in front of the burrito cooler.

"I told you to back off. We need to be socially distant."

"So your response when I got too close was to slap my dinner out of my hand? Food is scarce these days."

"I think you will be fine, bitch. You need to respect space. I don't want to get sick because of you."

"Well, you aren't exactly staying six feet away right now."

"Fuck you."

"No! Fuck you!"

They pause momentarily and look at me. I point to the burrito cooler. I'm ignored, and the fight continues.

"You are going to pay for this."

"You didn't even pay for it yet, and I know you can afford it, anyway."

"How do you know that?"

"The rock on your finger."

"This is my grandmother's."

"Well, she has shit for taste."

"She is dead."

"Good."

"What the hell did you just say?"

"I said your dead grandmother had terrible taste in rings."

"What is wrong with the ring?"

"For one, that beautiful diamond needs to be polished. Second, you can have it reset so it doesn't fall apart."

"Really? I was thinking the same thing."

"Yeah, honey. Here . . ." She reaches out and grabs the other woman's hand. "You can get this reset, and it will definitely honor your grandmother. I know a great jeweler you can go to. He is doing special appointments during the pandemic."

"It's like you are reading my mind."

"I got you, girl. I actually had my ring refurbished a little while back." She holds up her hand.

"Oh my! That's so very lovely. Okay, so I have to ask . . . where did you get that gorgeous silk shawl?"

I step forward and ask, "Hi, can I just grab a burrito from behind you?"

They look at me and then return to their conversation.

"Oh, it's from this little boutique around the way," she replies to the woman's question without acknowledging my existence.

I'm not wearing anything that reveals that I work at Dream Grocers. I decide to walk around them and lean over to get a burrito. I accidentally brush one of them.

"Excuse me. What the hell are you doing? Social distance."

"I already asked for you to move. I need to eat."

"Social distance!"

"Listen, I am just grabbing a burrito. And you are standing two feet from a woman as you comment on her lovely scarf."

"Social distance!"

"Hypocrite," I mutter.

The other woman joins in with a resounding "Social distance!"

Everyone is looking at me now with judging eyes peering over their masks. A person who was not involved screams, "Social distance!"

Then another.

A choir of people begin to chant, "Social distance! Social distance! Social distance!"

Panicked and afraid of how this might turn out, I walk away, their voices fading behind me. I look back to see them pointing as they confer about me.

The first person I run into is Lila.

"You okay? You look flustered," she says with a sweet smile hidden but still visible behind her mask.

"Yeah. I'm alright. I just had a weird interaction with some Lindas about a burrito and keeping my social distance."

"Huh?"

"Never mind. People are just starting to act really strange."

"Are you surprised?"

"You know, I guess I'm not. I'm just disappointed that people can't be more consistent. One minute everyone is calling us heroes, and in the next breath, they won't let me have a burrito for lunch."

"That sounds like normal humans to me. In a way, I like what's going on. People are just revealing who they really are. They're inconsistent, scared, irrational, self-involved beings that don't really know what to do when the veil is lifted."

"Don't you think that is a bit dark? I mean, I generally like people."

"Oh no, it's not a bad thing. It makes me love people even more. We are natural and flawed, and it's beautiful."

"You always say the right things, Lila. Why can't I have a perspective like you?"

"You do, Daniel."

"I do?" I respond, slightly confused.

"Yes, you do. You just need to lean into it and let go."

"Let go of what?"

"The way you think things are or are supposed to be."

"Everyone at this store has such deep perspectives. It feels like I am working with gurus like Tony Robbins."

If I am honest with myself, I fit right in with all of these wandering souls. The store is a magnet for people who like to watch and participate in humanity as opposed to only going through the motions. Lila is right. I need to let go. And every moment I spend in this store, I'm shedding the old me little by little.

"That's what happens when you live with your life on the grocery line."

"Life on the grocery line, eh? I like it."

"I have a feeling that people are going to forget what happened here like they always do."

"Oh, they definitely will. I should have added *forgetful* to the list of attributes I see in humans—now, during the pandemic, more than ever."

As I speak those words, Linda One and Linda Two who yelled at me about social distancing walk by as if nothing happened.

"Those are the women who yelled at me when I got a burrito."

"We are forgotten," Lila replies with zero visible emotion.

Mike walks up to me and Lila. "Hey, Daniel, did you get in a confrontation with some women about social distancing?"

"Jesus. That just happened. How the hell? And they just walked by. But yeah, I was trying to get a burrito for my lunch, and the women were standing in front of the cooler. I brushed up to one after they ignored my polite request that they move. They started freaking out on me, so I just walked away."

"Ah, I see. Well, they saw you talking to Lila and brought it up with the store manager. He might talk to you about the incident today. Just be aware."

"Really? I have only been here a week. I'm still on my probationary period. I'm trying my best. I didn't even talk to those women. Well, I guess I did say . . ."

"Shit, man, what did you say?" Mike asks.

"Never mind. I doubt they heard it."

Mike relaxes and says, "I'm sure it's nothing. He's a pretty good guy. He understands where we are coming from on these things."

"But it's a pandemic. No one is thinking straight right now."

"Relax, hon," Lila says. "You will be fine."

"I think putting this temp gun on employees' heads for a few hours is messing with my mind."

"Want to go to the front door to switch it up?" Mike asks.

"Yes, please."

"Okay. Give me a few minutes," Mike replies.

"Good luck," beautiful Lila says as she walks away.

"God, I want to marry her someday," I say to Mike.

He smiles back. "You and everyone else, little brother."

* * *

Halfway through my shift, Mike moves me to the front door of the building. He hands me a counter and tells me that it's one way in and one way out for the customers.

"How did they get this plan together so fast?"

Mike shrugs. "Who knows?"

"Yeah, I guess it's not a very sophisticated plan. But it will have to do. How many are allowed in the store at once?"

"Eighty people."

"People are gonna be really mad having to wait in line. Especially if it starts snowing."

"Yeah. It's not our fault, though, so just go with it."

The line wraps around almost the entire building. And just yesterday there was a free flow of people in and out of any entrance at the front of the store. I sit under a canopy, sheltered from a bleak, overcast March day, and observe the parking lot full of Mercedes Benz G-Wagens, Tesla Model Xs, Porsche Cayennes, and BMW M5s. The unabated sound of helicopter blades oscillates as background noise. Occasionally, I see a Maserati or a Bentley, but for the most part, my store is a false flag of wealth. Our customers are overpaying for a proper place in our social structure. People are lying to us. Their lies telling the world about self-worth fester like open wounds as they tremble in the crisp spring air.

But nonetheless, I sit here counting people as they come in and out of the building. Customers stand silently nearby, slouching with arms folded, in forty-degree temperatures that don't allow for one to remain comfortable. I don't have a heater. My fingers are frozen to the little circular tally counter. We give out masks to anyone who isn't wearing one. Everyone has their masks except for one man.

I ask Trevor, my fellow parking-lot attendant. "Dude, how did they get masks so fast? This is the first I'm even hearing of a mask mandate."

"I have no idea, man."

"I wonder why no one seems to know anything."

"I'm too cold to worry about it."

"I guess you're right."

Three people exit the building. "Okay. I can let in three." As the third person passes, the maskless man keeps walking, as though he is going to enter.

I hold up my hand to get his attention. "Sorry, sir, we are at capacity. We are only allowed to have eighty customers in at a time to keep social distancing a priority."

"Seriously? I just need to grab one thing."

"I'm sorry. I can't. It's a city regulation. Also, do you have a mask?"

"Those assholes. No, I don't have a mask. I don't see the point to all of this bullshit."

"I see. Well, we require a mask to go into the store. Here, you can use this one."

He stares in silent disgust.

I have been here less than a week, but I've learned that when people stare at you after you answer their questions, it is usually because they want to break you. They are waiting for you to give in to their attempted tyranny. But they do that because they are weak and they have no access to the power they want. If this guy wants to, he could walk right past me, and I could do nothing to stop him. If I attempt to stop him, I could get fired, and the customer could sue the store. He is putting on an air of strength, but really, he is just a coward.

"Alright, someone just walked out. You can go in."

He puts the mask on as he walks in and slides it under his chin. The gentleman behind him walks up and says, "What a douche."

"All day, every day," I respond, even though this is actually the first time I have dealt with any of this type of behavior.

"You all don't get paid enough for this shit."

"Sacrifices must be made," I reply.

"If you ask me, y'all seem to be the sacrificial lambs here," he says as he walks in the store.

Trevor and I look at each other.

"Well, that was weird," he says.

"No kidding. So you have been here since the morning, right?" I ask Trevor.

"Yeah, and it's been miserable the whole time."

"I can imagine. Why don't we have a space heater?"

"Cheap fucks," Trevor blurts out.

"It's the bottom line, my friend," I respond.

"Eh. I'm just kidding. The heater is on the way. Mike went to grab us one," Trevor says with a laugh.

Undeterred, I go into a small rant. "Well, fuck their bottom line . . . oh wait . . . okay. Great. Hopefully he will be here soon. But I'll still say what I was going to originally. If you treat your employees poorly, your customers will be treated in a similar manner."

"True, true, but at least we have some power here."

"What do you mean?"

"We get to choose who goes in and out. We are the gatekeepers. And we have a cop to back us up. Huh, Rory?"

"Oh hell yeah! I got your back," Rory, the cop standing by, replies.

"I appreciate your enthusiasm," I say.

"Ah, fuck, man. I hate these entitled fools. They are the worst. Anything I can do to help make their lives less cushioned, the better."

"Hear! Hear! Maybe you can help us fight off all the old folks who love the small carts," Trevor says.

"Hear! Hear!" I reply.

"Small carts?" Rory asks.

"Just wait, man, you will see. Old people love those two-tier small carts. And they ask about them all the damn time."

I scan the line for a certain type of face and say, "See. I bet that lady that's fourth in line asks for a small cart."

"I was just thinking she was all about them," Trevor replies. "Good thing I haven't grabbed any from the parking lot in an hour or two."

"Really? Like on purpose?" I ask.

"Yeah, man. We only have a few, and it's a futile effort to go through. Plus, there is a select cross section of folks that are adamant about getting their small cart and are never polite about it. It's fun to piss them off. So fuck 'em."

I laugh at the beauty of his jab to the Lindas and Daves of the world. "I applaud your efforts, brother."

"Gotta do what you can. And I find it really entertaining."

Rory responds, "I second that."

Soon enough, the woman I called out steps to the front of the line. Her skin looks of an old catcher's glove drenched in rejuvenating oils meant to revive glory years. She looks around momentarily and loudly demands, "Where are the goddamn small carts?"

"I'm sorry. We don't have any right now," I respond.

"Well, why the hell not?" she fires back as her evident rage builds.

"We only have about ten of the carts, and they are really popular. People steal them for some reason."

"Why don't you get more of them?"

Humor turns to frustration. It's been a long day of people and their goddamn American tragedies. I respond in almost a sweet tone, "I'm not sure, ma'am. You could talk to the management about it."

"Why don't you talk to the management about it?" she blurts out and storms off into the store.

Because, lady, I don't care. No one cares. Don't you realize there's a pandemic going on? Or do you not care because your family doesn't talk to you anymore? You should be grateful you aren't on a respirator, dying, all alone.

I don't say that, of course. I take the high road and hold my tongue. Part of a customer-service job is regulating emotions, subduing that internal dialogue, and being the better person. But one reward that comes from being paid to deal with the public is knowing that in those moments where they lambast me with all of their insecurities and loneliness, they fail at keeping it together, but I keep my composure like a stoic emperor facing the tyranny of small carts. We all lose our shit from time to time. And there are justified moments for anyone to be upset. This incident was not one of them. She didn't earn sympathy or empathy from her behavior.

People who are good at customer service should receive a medal. Correction: *I* should receive a medal. Or we should get to push over an old lady who treats us like pieces of shit.

Because I don't give a good rat's ass about the small carts. And most people are polite. They find out we don't have many, and then they move on with their lives. They don't shit on strangers because they are miserable.

If I had a small cart, I would find a person infected with COVID-19 and have them cough all over it so you could rest your ancient frame as you walk around and pick out your organic watermelon radishes as you slowly get infected. Sure, we both would be exposed, but I would get two weeks off paid and survive. You might make it through. I'm not sure. I kinda hope not. Jesus. Fucking. Christ. Calm down, dude.

Once I snap back into reality, I look over at Trevor and Rory. They are both laughing hysterically.

Trevor says, "Man, she really got after you. I could see the fire in your eyes, bro. I'm surprised you didn't snap back."

"Who would win if I did that?"

"Well, good point there, Zen master. Should we go get some small carts from the parking lot?"

"Nah. Let them suffer."

"You know they could overrun us if they wanted to," Trevor says in between laughter.

"But they won't."

"What makes you so sure? Civility?"

"Fear."

"Fear of what?"

"Of what the caged animals who shop here might do. Most people don't know what it is to be desperate. We aren't there yet, of course, but it's a terrifying place to be."

"You are so wise, my brother," Trevor says. He stands up and moves into a striker pose and says, "Wax on, wax off."

"Sorry, this hangover has me rambling."

"I think you've got a point," Rory interjects. "I mean, I see that type of fear all of the time—that desperation. You see it in drug addicts. They've hit that point where nothing will stop them from getting what they want and need. These people in the line aren't there yet. Hell, they are shopping at a Dream Grocers during the 'end times.' Everything here costs five times what it does at a normal grocery store. They can still buy their way out of this situation. Or so they think."

"Wow. Okay. We need to calm down all the serious talk. It's depressing enough out here. No need to bring us all down," says Trevor.

"Yeah, Rory," I reply.

"Get it together, Rory," Trevor continues.

"Hey, man . . . I'm just trying to teach you boys about reality."

"I'm thirty, man. I've seen some shit," I say.

"Nah. Just wait, young man. Wait until the riots come," Rory replies.

Rory is a good-natured fella with some gray hair and an easygoing manner. He isn't who I would expect to be a police officer. He shares weird stories about drug arrests gone awry and carries a pretty anti-authority vibe with him. The drug war is always up for debate. I enjoy our talks. Today, we have been chatting about the civil unrest that has taken hold in our city since the lockdown. Buildings are burning. Crime is on the rise. It's been only one fucking day. That's terrifying.

"What did we say, dude? No negativity. My edible is starting to kick in, and we can't have negative vibes," Trevor says with a smile.

"Sorry, guys."

"Don't worry about him, man. Speak your truth," I say.

"Okay, well, the riots are coming," Rory continues. "Just you wait."

"Alright, Rory. Alright," I say in a tone meant to relieve the tension. "Now, can we go back to talking shit about old rich people wanting small carts?"

"That's what I've been saying, man. Remember when that lady almost took your head off over the little carts?" Trevor pleads.

"You mean five minutes ago?"

"Sure. I just want to make sure you aren't still shaken up."

"Nah, dude. I'm fine."

"You sure? I mean, you are saying one thing, but I'm picking up different vibes."

"That's because you are high at work, Trevor."

"Does everyone get high and go to work here?" asks Rory.

"Yup, that's life on the grocery line. It's a coping mechanism."

"Hear! Hear!" I reply.

"Hear! Hear!" says Trevor.

"I don't know if I should be talking about this with you two. I work in narcotics, you know?" Rory says.

"We know," I say.

"And you don't care?"

"It's a coping mechanism, man."

"The weed or not caring?"

"Both."

"Apathy swingeth a huge sword," Trevor says, widening his bloodshot eyes.

"Pride goeth before small carts. Amen," I reply.

Rory stares at us, then bursts out laughing and says, "Well, at least you two are entertaining."

"And I'm not even high," I respond.

"Really?"

"Yes sir. This is just my natural disposition."

Rory peers at me momentarily, then replies with an uncertain "Hmm."

The banter continues like this for some time as we wave the keys to the preservation of society in the customers' faces. I am learning that the only option is to laugh hard and often. The glossy version of civility that I'm used to is rife with fear and anxiety. Talking shit with coworkers and cops is the best way to process the madness.

I scroll through Twitter like a junky as I count people going in and out. I don't really care about the count. With every doom-scroll of my smartphone, I see that terrible things are happening everywhere. People are losing their minds. Rory was wrong about one thing: riots aren't coming *soon*. They are already here. Even these people in line are participating in a silent, condoned looting of the store.

Once inside, let the hoarding begin. As I walk to the break room, I see shelves ravaged and stripped bare. The expected items such as pasta, rice, canned food of any sort, and bottled water are all gone. But it doesn't stop there. Toilet paper and paper towels are nowhere to be found. Any and all bottled beverages such as lemonade and cold-pressed juices are gone. The meat department looks like a pack of wolves had their way on both the food and the employees. Even the dairy and produce departments look like a tornado ran through. You can't freeze-dry organic unpasteurized milk. What is the point here? Decision-making seems to be unraveling in real time. Every glance I catch carries with it a hollow look of uncertainty. There is a buzz to the store. Or maybe it's more of a roar, like a wave about to crash and break the spirits of every person in the room.

On my break, I watch a video of one woman attempting to gouge another's eyes for bumping into her in line at a Walgreens. She does this as her children look on in horror. They went at it for thirty seconds or so until it was broken up by security. But the irony is that no one was wearing a mask, and wrestling around on the ground isn't exactly social distancing. There is video after video after video of similar behavior by people in power condemning one side or the other. No one is trying to calm people down. All I see is a fanning of the flames.

I am grateful that I haven't had to deal with such madness, but it seems inevitable that I will at some point. It's going to get worse before it gets better.

I make my way to the bathroom and stand in front of the mirror and pull my skin tightly, checking for new moles, examining my receding hairline, and wondering what I can do to soften the bags that have developed under my eyes—I will do anything to make this moment last longer. I just need more time before I go back, and if I claim I was in the bathroom, they won't have reason to argue. Thirty years has never felt so old. I massage my jawline because TMJ has been acting up since I put on the mask. Seconds feel like minutes as I examine the weight and dexterity of my own personal Vietnam. I know this is nothing compared to war, but it's definitely a big moment to all of those on the front lines. I'm in the middle of something too big and laborious to comprehend—not only for my fellow essential workers but also for the world at large. Countries of all sizes will never be the same. And all I want to do is work from my computer at home like I did in a previous life. I would gladly go back to the Pajama Class and work in sweatpants. Why do I feel so fucking old right now?

* * *

Trevor and Rory are gone, and I am monitoring the front by myself until my replacement gets here. The cool air has given way to a surprisingly hot afternoon. Springtime weather in the Rocky Mountains is temperamental, but I sit in relative comfort on my throne with a fan blowing on me.

There is still a line wrapped around the building. I stagger the steady stream of Lindas and Daves who want provisions from my store.

Billy, another coworker older than me but young in spirit, arrives. He looks annoyed to be here.

"You okay with me going on a few cart runs?" he asks.

"Sounds good to me."

A mirage shimmers as water evaporates from the sun-drenched asphalt. I watch Billy move across the parking lot in his neon-orange vest with yellow stripes and bright-white sneakers. I would hold no ill will to see him crawl on top of a BMW M5 like a lizard on a rock to bake the day away under the sun as it roasts our suburban enclave. After all, the rich are getting restless, and these people will drive anyone to the brink of madness when they are caught outside their comfort zone.

We have been at capacity all day. And I see at least ten people exiting their cars to enter the building.

I've settled into my role as the person doing the counting and handing out masks. I silently wish for us to dip below the magic number of eighty people allowed inside at once. Relief would be nice, but it's unlikely and rare at our store. We are one of the busiest in the tri-state area. People love the decadence of our selection—whether it's organic, free range, free trade, locally sourced, handpicked, or any other number of buzzwords. We have the luxury to sustain our upper-middle-class clientele.

Without warning, everyone from the parking lot arrives at once, including Billy. The line doubles instantly. People exist in anger and boredom simultaneously as they stand with their arms crossed, wishing for the experience to be over. I try my best to direct people in and out. My head is on a swivel as I herd cats into our high-end grocery-store fun house.

Will this go on all day, every day, during the pandemic? I have a sneaking suspicion it will. Sometimes it's mundane; other times I enjoy myself and the small amount of power it affords me to tell people what they can and can't do. Self-aggrandizement of my importance matched with self-immolation of the soul are all I have during the viral fog. And I will take what I can get during these thieving political times.

Billy points to two women in line. "Oh boy! Here they come. Jackie and Gina have arrived. These women are a trip. Just wait."

Jackie and Gina reach the front of the line. I'm told these women are regulars. Billy recognizes them from the remnants of early plastic surgery they display on their faces, alligator-skin handbags, and an obvious benzodiazepine-and-wine deportment as they stand in luxurious tennis clothes. He says they are in our store at least five times a week. They stop through after tennis. It boggles my mind to know people shop every day in a store that charges at least 50 percent more per item than other supermarkets.

"Okay. You two can go in," I say as I motion for them to enter.

One of the women is struggling to put on her mask. "It doesn't go on your forehead, honey," her friend says with a giggle as she casually licks an ice-cream cone.

"Well, help me, goddamnit."

"Oh, honey, you are beyond help. But you will get it eventually," the woman says, followed by another lick of the ice cream.

I notice the ice-cream woman isn't trying to put on a mask, and I say, "Umm . . . ma'am . . . ma'am! You will need a mask to go into the store."

"Oh, I'm not going in, honey," she responds. "See . . . here . . . goddamnit . . . hold still." The woman with the ice-cream cone pulls her friend's mask down

143

over her mouth. "Isn't that better? Now, remember we need cheese for our wine." The masked woman nods in agreement and goes into the store. Her mask with some law firm's name on it is upside down, but I decide not to say anything.

The other woman steps out of the line and moves toward Billy, me, and Rory. I can hear her slurping on the ice cream.

"Have you heard of Ray's Ice Cream around the corner? It's the best. Simply the best."

"No, I haven't," I respond, noticing out of the corner of my eye that another person in line is not wearing a mask. "Excuse me, sir. You have to wear a mask to go in."

"Oh yeah, I forgot mine. Do you have extras?"

"Of course. Here you go."

"Well, it's owned by the nicest negro man," Jackie says.

"It's owned by . . . wait, what?"

"Ray. He is a negro man. He is the sweetest man, and he makes the best ice cream."

I look over at Billy and Rory. I look back at Jackie, who is standing in all white, grooming the half-melted soft-serve ice cream down to a nub as she talks into a vacuum about all things she considers important in her life. She hasn't skipped a beat. She doesn't seem to be talking to anyone but herself. None of her words register with me, and no one is *listening* with any intention. Billy and the cop stare in clear astonishment.

I only start to digest her words when she says, "You know, at our tennis club, everyone uses the same tennis balls, and no one has gotten sick. Not a soul. I mean, I don't think it's that big of a deal, really. You know, the mask thing. It's kind of upsetting."

Billy leans in and whispers, "What the fuck is she talking about?"

"Her perspective," I answer.

"She seems lost."

"I know . . . in utter isolation. Man, I could use some ice cream."

"Me too."

Gina walks out of the exit with a nice paper bag. Jackie yells, "Did you get the cheese and chocolate?"

"Of course. Wait, what chocolate?"

"You forgot the chocolate? Shit. Oh, honey."

"Geez . . . I'm just kidding, sweetie. You really need to lay off the wine. It's right here."

"What a bitch! You boys see what I have to deal with?"

Jackie is trying to get more of my attention, but I've had enough. So I ignore her.

"Alright, sister," Gina says. "Let's go. Goodbye, boys!"

* * *

The evening arrives. My teeth are chattering, and I am unable to catch my breath because of the windchill.

"Did they get the heater yet?" I ask Billy.

"Not yet, man. Are you okay? You don't look so great."

"Well, I was supposed to be off hours ago. I know I'm getting overtime, but shit, man. I didn't expect to close."

Mike walks out with the heater.

"Here ya go, man," Mike says. "Sorry it took so long. Thanks again for staying."

"No problem. Anything for Dream Grocers."

He smiles. "What a long day, and it's supposed to snow for the next few days."

"Damn. We don't need snow and cold. We need sunshine and laughter. Any other news?"

"About what?"

"The virus, the lockdown, the riots. Anything."

"I'm not sure. I haven't looked at my phone in a long time. You two out here have a better chance than me."

"You're okay with that?"

"Of course. You are the ones freezing your asses off out here," Mike says and heads back in.

I look at my phone. "Looks like they are locking down everything for the next few weeks. Only things that will be open are essential services."

"What does *essential services* mean?"

"Well, grocery stores for one."

"Duh, what else? Hopefully, bars will remain open."

"Nope, bars and restaurants will be closed."

"Seriously?"

"Yup. Drink up now while you still can."

"No kidding. That's the only way I can get away from my kids."

"I thought you loved being a father."

"Yeah, but everyone needs an escape. I can't be with the kids all the time."

"Well, you still have me," I say with a smirk.

"That's great. So. Fucking. Great."

"It says here that we are only expecting a six-week shutdown. You can handle that, right?"

"I guess so. Will liquor stores still be open?"

"Looks like it."

"Yeah, I'll be able to get through with the help of Jameson and Rolling Rock."

"Sounds reasonable."

"We all need to make sacrifices."

"For the greater good. I'm glad everything is healthy at the Billy household. Should we start closing up?"

"Sure. I'll get the carts," Billy replies.

"What are we going to do with this line around the building? We need to close soon. Can you grab Mike and see what we should do?" I ask.

Billy comes back after a minute or so and says, "He said just tell them we open tomorrow at six a.m. We need time to restock."

"Oh, that's going to go well."

"They will just have to deal. Restaurants are still open right now. These people will be fine."

"Ha. We shall see," I reply, then turn to the line. "Hi, everyone! Excuse me. I have an announcement." The frustrated crowd turns to me, and I say, "We are closing for the night. We will open tomorrow at six a.m." As I say this, I realize Rory isn't close, and the yelling begins.

"Like hell you are! I didn't wait in line for twenty minutes to go home empty handed. I am going in."

"Me too!"

"Yeah! Fuck that! I am going in too."

I'm looking at approximately thirty people. I glance around. Billy is off getting carts. Rory is nowhere to be found. The yelling continues. I double down. "I'm sorry, but we must close. We need time to restock the shelves. I apologize for the inconvenience."

"You apologize for the inconvenience? Fuck you, man! You aren't inconvenienced at all. You can go in and start shopping after the doors close. I have a family to feed. I'm getting in here."

He begins to move toward the door. It's locked.

"The door is locked, sir."

"Well, you better let me in, motherfucker."

He lunges forward. I move quickly to the side, and he falls down. Before he can recover, I put my boot into his face. The crowd gasps. A few of them are filming me with their phones.

Rory comes running up. "Are you okay?" he asks. "I was grabbing a burrito for dinner, and I heard the commotion."

"I'm fine. This asshole tried to fight me."

"Are you going to get in trouble for this?" Rory asked.

"That's a good question."

* * *

I leave that night thinking I'm going to be fired and possibly sued. The towering corporation that hired me doesn't tolerate retaliations against customers, even if justified and in self-defense. It's one of those backward aspects of capitalism that ends up rewarding bad behavior.

When I arrive home, I find some of my neighbors huddled around a bottle of whiskey, sitting on the community patio.

"Hey, man, how was work?" Jason asks. "Whoa. Dude. You don't look so great!"

"Believe me; I don't feel so great. Today was terrifying, long, humiliating, gratifying. It was everything, really. All the emotions wrapped into one."

"I can imagine. Do you want a drink?"

"Pour it strong, man. I need to put my bag in my apartment and change real quick."

"Sounds good. It will be ready for you."

When I return to the patio, I begin to hear peculiar sounds coming from every angle. People are howling like wolves—loud and with a wave of solidarity—my neighbors join in, and so do I when I reach the patio. Aarhh-woooooooooo! Arh-arh-woooooooooo! Demons are dropping to the floor from the deafening sound as we guffaw deep into the night. I lift my glass as if to cheer my fellow suffering fools. "Why are we doing this?" I ask.

"It's to show our solidarity with essential workers," Jason replies, then stops and gives a short pause. "Sorry, man. I forgot."

"Don't be sorry. I'm glad people are caring about 'essential workers.'"

"Me too. So does this mean we should be howling at you?"

I laugh. "No, but I will take another glass of whiskey."

"Deal."

Knowing that we are howling for essential workers does feel kind of disingenuous. Like what are we *actually* doing? It's the same thing as calling someone a hero for going to work. Or is that just the long day getting me down? At least people care, for now. Maybe this will carry on into the future and we will be better for it. The sounds of human-wolves subside, and we sit down in our chairs.

"Man, it's cold out here. I heard it's going to snow," Jason says with a shiver.

"Yeah, I heard the same thing. It feels so lonely when the snow falls."

"But you aren't alone. We are here."

"True. But you guys aren't here all of the time, and the city is so quiet now. I can still hear those damn helicopters, but I can never see them," I reply.

"They are circling around the capitol. Protests and riots have started picking up. Buildings are burning."

"No shit? That's crazy."

"I know. Before you got home, we were listening to more neighbors."

"Anything interesting happen?"

"Well, we think we heard a couple fighting. I think it was that pregnant couple across the alley. He was yelling at her, and she said something about the baby. But then the howling started."

Loud sirens rush down the street next to the patio. Levy pauses and says, "All I've heard lately are ambulances and sirens. I never hear the cars passing by."

"Yeah, along with the helicopters, it's creepy. It just feels like there is an invisible emergency going on, but we can't see. I can't shake the feeling something is wrong," Jason says.

I respond, "On my ride home there weren't any cars on the street. Same yesterday. I rode against the grain on major streets, just waiting for car lights to appear over each tiny hill."

"Sounds like a bad acid trip."

"I mean, yes and no. There is something both beautiful and tragic in the absence of other humans. I get to be alone with my thoughts, but it's hard to be alone with your thoughts."

"Well, there is always the internet, where you are never alone," Jason says with a laugh.

I shake my head. "Oh god. That's where the downfall of humanity will happen."

"It's definitely where the next revolution will happen," Jason states confidently.

"I don't know, man," I say. "This whole thing is going to cause civil unrest and backlash for years to come. Anyway, what are our neighbors talking about?"

We go quiet and listen for a moment.

"Do you hear those voices? They sound like kids talking," Levy says.

"Yeah, I do." I look around. The voices are very light, but I wonder if we will be able to see them. "Hey, look over there. Is that them?" I say, pointing to a close apartment kitty-corner from ours.

"That's definitely two kids playing a video game. But wouldn't we hear the TV?"

"Ah, true. But do you wonder what they are talking about?"

"They are probably just talking shit to people over the internet."

"People they probably don't even know in person. That's the future generation."

"You're right. That's how kids interact now."

"Do you think this pandemic will normalize that even more?" I wonder aloud.

"Yeah. Probably. I hadn't thought of that. But so what? Our parents didn't understand us either. The older generation never understands the next one."

I nod. "I agree, but people are still social creatures. We need person-to-person contact. Depression is going to skyrocket because of this pandemic. Just wait. Kids need to play and socialize in person. It's vital."

"I agree, but this isn't temporary."

"It's supposed to be." I shrug. "I don't believe that in six weeks it will 'flatten the curve' or whatever. I think we will be dealing with this until we die."

"Of the virus? Highly unlikely. It's mostly dangerous to the elderly and those with comorbidities."

"Oh no, I mean until we die of old age or an asteroid hits the planet. The implications of this pandemic will never leave us. Or we will forget it is around, even though it has infected everything in our life."

"What about if and when they get a vaccine?"

"Then there will be another coronavirus and another. On and on. It's always going to be something that is trying to kill us. Now that we have the internet and we are integrated into the system, we can't go back. Jesus, I'm sorry," I apologize. "This whiskey has crawled all over me."

"It's fine, man. I mean, you're making sense. You are seeing the madness firsthand. The rest of us are just watching it on YouTube or Twitter. Should we bark for you?"

"If you insist."

"Aarh-aarh-wooooooo!"

I join in the chorus, and it feels glorious. "Arah-woooooooooooo! Arah-woooooooooooo!"

Chapter Seven

I arrive at work welcomed by a huge line that wraps around the building, with Lindas and Daves staggered roughly six feet apart under an overcast sky with a slight breeze blowing south. I walk through the temperature-check station. Lila puts a gun to my head with an unseen smile and says, "You are good to go."

"Is that what it will be like when we get married?" I ask while giving a slight smile that I'm sure she can feel.

"From the get-go. You still have my number, right?"

"Yes."

"Then use it."

"I'll text you tonight."

As I walk past the registers, I see a Norman without his mask talking to a cashier. I can see the droplets of spit hitting the plexiglass. The employee is wincing as he speaks. I look back at Lila. She is watching the same thing. She walks over to the man while standing six feet away and politely asks for him to put on a mask.

"I don't have to!" the customer insists. "It's my goddamn right to not wear a mask."

"I understand that, sir, but we require it in the store, and it's polite."

"That's bullshit. I'm done here anyway," he says and storms off.

She looks back at me, pulls down her mask, and mouths the words "All day."

When I get upstairs, a group of people are standing around looking at a message on the whiteboard by the time clock that reads:

Please note we will be closing early for the next two weeks due to ongoing protests. This is just a precautionary measure due to the recent violence. It's not a political statement. We are just being cautious.

"Bullshit, it's not a political statement," a coworker blurts out.

"It's business, dude," another responds.

"Business is political," a third voice yells.

"Well, it shouldn't be," I mumble to myself.

"It always will be," Alejandro whispers; then he leans in and says, "What's up, brother?"

"Not much, man. Just dying on the vine."

"I feel ya. How long is your shift today?"

"No idea. It seems to change every day."

"Yeah, they approved overtime. So enjoy it while it lasts."

"I don't know if *enjoy* is a word I would use to describe overtime."

"Ah, true. When did you start?"

"Last Monday."

"Seriously?"

"Yup. Hell of a way to start a job, huh?"

"Yeah, dude. You've swallowed a lifetime of shit in seven days. Hell, you sound like a grizzled veteran coming home from his second tour in Afghanistan."

"Except my battlefield is consoling oil-fortune heiresses about the fact that their cat might have coronavirus because their Dave of a husband doesn't care."

"Pets can carry the virus?" Alejandro asks.

"That's the rumor."

"Jesus, it's just one thing after the other."

"Over and over again, man."

There are grumblings among the group beginning, so Alejandro and I read on.

Do not be alarmed but we have had one person test positive for the virus. If you have any questions please contact management.

We are working with local officials to ensure everyone's safety. That is why it's very important for all of us to wear our PPE and practice social distancing. You all are doing a great job! Thank you for all your hard work. We know these are increasingly difficult times. If you have any questions or just need to talk to someone please reach out to your department lead.

"Who tested positive for the virus?" I ask Alejandro.

"Someone said it might be Tina."

"Damn, man. Was there anyone else exposed?"

"The managers are looking at the tapes right now."

"Well, I'm glad I didn't hang out with Tina the other night when everyone got together."

"Everyone got together? Like who?"

"Oh, just the regular crew. It was Tina's goddaughter's birthday. Weren't you invited?"

"No, I wasn't, which seems odd," he responds with a somber gaze. The realization hits me . . .

"Sorry, dude. I forgot you're her cousin. Sorry. I didn't mean to start any issues between you two. I'm sure you didn't really miss out on anything."

"That's my little cousin's goddaughter's birthday, man. Did you know Tina before?"

"No, but her and I hit it off, and we are becoming good friends."

"Jesus Christ. Well, I gotta find out what's going on."

"I get where you are coming from, homie, but could you not mention my name when you talk to her?" I ask.

"Sure. I'm sorry to get all heated, man; I just thought I would be invited. I mean, I visited her in the hospital when she had the baby, and I haven't seen her for a week or more. I've been worried."

"Umm . . . you know it's her goddaughter and not her actual child, right?"

"Oh? Well, still, fuck that. Her and I are going to have words."

Awkwardly, I try to change the subject. "Anyway, don't you hate these new rules?"

"Not really. I mean, they are just trying to keep us safe."

"It seems more like a frantic scramble and overreaction."

"Give them some time. I'm sure they will figure it out."

"Just like they figured out that plexiglass thing?" I respond, becoming increasingly agitated.

"I'm actually glad they did that. I read that it's transmitted through the air and by your hands," he replies.

"I can't hear the customers when they talk. It's frustrating, is all. Are they going to make us wipe down everything?"

"Yup. Between every customer too."

"That's gonna make everything take forever."

"It's a government mandate."

"On what grounds?"

He shrugs and says, "Safety first."

"Yeah, safety, that must be it."

"Listen, man, I will see you down there. I need to give Tina a call."

I have a few minutes before I need to go downstairs. There is a balcony overlooking the store, where I peer out at a maze filled with masked zombies of all shapes and sizes frantically searching for items to sustain their families. They are spooked. I can see they are avoiding each other and giving deep disdain-filled glares at people who come too close.

People are lined up all the way to the back of the store. Everyone is moving their limbs and rocking back and forth, wrought with nervous energy. And they are trying to remain socially distant at the same time. What a strange dance composed of fear and necessity, like "The Endtimes Waltz." I'm looking at a kettle ready to blow in real time.

As disturbing as the scene below strikes me as, it looks all too distant. I watch the human animal from outside its enclosure, detached, careful not to tap the glass, and then I move on and walk down the steps to meet whatever fresh version of hell I will experience next.

* * *

When I get down to the register, I see Mike working at the customer-service desk.

"Hey, dude," I say, "I am really sorry about the incident last night."

He looks up with a blank stare. "What incident?"

"The one where I kicked a guy in the face."

"You did *what?*" he responds in evident shock.

"Well, this guy was arguing with me, then . . ." Nothing is registering with Mike. I stop midsentence. "You have no idea what I am talking about, do you?"

"No. But now I assume you are assaulting our customers in your dreams. I do that, too, from time to time. It's natural in this line of work." He laughs.

"I guess it must have happened in a dream. It felt so real, though."

"It does, and it's wonderful. Just don't let it happen in real life. We like you working here way too much."

"I appreciate that. What is my register?"

"Hop on register four, and tell Lila to come over and talk to me before she goes on break."

"Okay. No problem."

I walk over to register four. Lila is standing there looking as beautiful as always. Across from her register is Christian, who puts up a peace sign when he notices that I am walking up. Mary walks by and reaches out with her elbow, to avoid the spreading of germs, because we aren't supposed to bump fists. I can tell she is smiling. Billy nods as he grabs baskets from behind the registers. Trevor is behind Lila. He points his finger to acknowledge me.

I tell Lila to go talk to Mike. She gladly leaves the register at my disposal. I know it's been only a week, but these semi-strangers are family to me. And I know that bonds forged by trauma aren't the strongest, but it doesn't matter, because family is a choice, and this is how I choose to deal.

I prepare bags for the next customer and look back into the herd of buffalo-like upper-middle-class Daves and Lindas seething for their chances to change my day and leave the store. I try to remember that I am a gate-keeper to a special place in society. And what I'm doing is important. But if these people are so afraid of things they have yet to understand, I fear the plexiglass won't save anyone and they will trample the fence and gate at will. In more ways than one, I am staring death in the face from both the novel coronavirus and the hungry, scared masses. My optimism is gone. I see now that this electric boogaloo is going to end in a dangerous fashion.

An all-too-familiar couple steps into my line. The "bro" with bloodshot, tear-rimmed eyes pushes his cart forward and begins unloading his groceries. There is a girl standing with her arms crossed behind him. Underneath her mask she is a ball of fury. If I were to guess, I'd say an argument happened not too long ago.

"Hello, how are you? Are you part of the Dream Team?"

"Nah, bro, we aren't," he says, sounding defeated.

"I would be careful with using the word *we* when you describe you and I," says the furious woman behind him.

"Babe, I am sorry," he whimpers.

"Again, no pet names for now. It's Lindy for you, David."

"Okay. Fine. What do you want me to say?"

"I want to know why you consider this our date night?"

"Well, babe . . . sorry, Lindy, there isn't anything else open right now."

"We could go to the damn park or something!" she pleads.

"It's snowing outside, babe."

"I don't know. You just need to figure it out."

"What do you want to do?"

"I want to go back to my normal life where my boy-friend, Davey, isn't such a fucking baby."

He redirects his conversation to me. "Do you see what I have to deal with here?"

Not sure what to say but trying to stay neutral, I reply, "Yeah. The pandemic is rough on everyone."

"Don't give him an excuse," she replies.

"Oh, I promise I'm not. By the way, you two look really familiar. Have you been in the store before?"

"We come in from time to time," the pretty girl replies.

"We all look the same with the masks on, man," the boyfriend fires back.

"That's true. But I swear you have gone through my line recently."

I say this with rising excitement. The chance to toy with these people makes me happy. My heart darkens. I want revenge, but I also pity these two fools.

"Not us, man."

The woman interjects. "Shut up, Davey. I'm sorry. He doesn't know anything."

"Babe, not in front of people," the man says.

"Shut the fuck up, baby Davey."

"Okay," I cut in. "No worries. I must have been mistaken."

"Oh, you're fine," she says. "He is just in the doghouse. I hope you have a great night, sweetie."

"Thanks. Have a good date night. See you soon."

"I sure hope so," she replies as her cheeks lift, indicating a smile. His shoulders droop as they both walk away. I can hear her talking as they pass. She glances back at me.

It's hard to watch anyone be flattened and humiliated in front of me, even if they probably deserve more suffering than they receive, because it's a pandemic, and I've been told a thousand times that we are all in it together. But when people say that phrase, are they including the couple that just went through my line? Because they don't strike me as people coming together for the common good. They are just in each other's way. What I see are humans who have let the good in them turn into rot and fill their relationship and their soul. And now it's exposed.

They were playing pretend in the game of life just a day or two ago. Everything was fine, and they were going to make it through. They mocked me as they made out in line. Now, it's over, as it should have been before it began. But people need their trial and error. And maybe she will forgive him, and he will buy her roses, and they will go back to a faux relationship instead of accepting the cracks in the foundation as a sign they are doomed.

The idea of having a date night at a grocery store leaves me wondering how this generation will turn out. The prospect isn't good when we look far enough down the line. Magnifying the faults but leaving them unresolved is not the best course of action when you are faced with a challenge such as a pandemic. But what the hell do I know? I'm a lowly "essential" cashier being slowly trampled by Lindas and Daves. My next customer is unloading her groceries, and I have little time to ponder the disintegration of millions of lives.

A young boy runs ahead of his parents through my checkout line. He unfolds the bags to prepare for the groceries to come down the conveyor belt. I'm not finished ringing up the customer ahead of them, so the little guy has to wait. My first thought is the parents need to control this child, especially since everyone is trying to practice social distancing. That infuriates me a little bit. I understand taking your kids out of the house because they are going crazy, but it's probably not a great idea to let them run around spreading germs. His parents bicker as I ask them my standard questions.

Once I'm finished ringing them up, I listen closely as I hand them a receipt.

The couple is fighting about things that don't directly correspond to the relationship. It's the kind of shit that lingers around until the breaking point. Close proximity to each other for far too long can do that to anyone.

"Well, you should get that kind of butter if you like it," the man says in a passive-aggressive tone.

"I don't want the butter," she responds, as if to drop the conversation altogether.

"You're going to need it for that bread you bought. You are the only one that will eat that shit. Get the butter." He turns to me, not waiting for her response, and asks, "Excuse me, sir, does she have time to run back and grab some butter?"

"Sure," I reply.

She sighs, then says, "Okay. I'll get the butter."

I'm no expert, but her taste in bread and butter isn't the problem. Maybe it is some deep-seated resentment about his failings as a husband? Or maybe he just knew that she would want that damn butter. Either way, he crushed her emotions right in front of me. And that can't be good. People have bad days, and it could be that I caught them in a tough moment. But how many shitty moments can happen before the shaky foundations on which people like this couple built their relationships crumble? There will be a large spike in children, like that little boy waiting to bag groceries, who will spend Christmas with Mommy and Thanksgiving with Daddy from now on.

I don't know what happened to my optimism. I'm not this person at all. I need to talk to Lila or Christian or Mike. There is comfort among those left in the trenches.

Linda is shaking as she unloads her groceries. Her husband asks if she needs help.

"Yes, babe. Can you please do it? I just don't know if I can . . . this is all too much."

"Of course, babe. We will make it through. Those death toll numbers are crazy."

"I have seen several articles saying at least four million dead."

I decide to chime in and ask, "Four million? That's a huge number."

Her look of annoyance is obvious—she isn't pleased that I decided to involve myself in their conversation. "Yes. They are saying it on all the major cable networks."

"Wow. I hope they are wrong," I reply. She ignores me and returns to their conversation.

"Babe, we need to trust the experts. They are looking out for us."

"I know, babe," he replies.

"So have you thought about what we should do tonight? It's our anniversary, after all."

"Oh, I know what I want to do tonight," he replies with a grin.

"Oh, babe, I don't know if we should do that right now. We want to reduce the spread, you know? We have to be careful. That virus is so contagious," she says with a giggle, then touches his arm.

"We will wear masks," he replies in a serious tone. "On the news they were saying it can lower your risk of transmission."

"Oh, that's kind of hot and fun."

"Well, like you said, we should trust the experts."

"Exactly, sounds fun either way. I'm down."

* * *

The day is winding down, but the line doesn't seem to be ending anytime soon. They *all* need the food we supply. I wonder how many of them wish they had been better friends or lovers or parents as they watch the world crumble. They get to reevaluate their entire lives while waiting to pay for pasta, toilet paper, canned crabmeat, and other luxurious Dream Grocers accommodations.

The next customer steps in front of me. He is wearing a driving cap and has piercing blue eyes. Wrapped around one of his eyes is a huge bruise. A cold chill runs down my spine.

"What happened to your eye?" I ask.

He stops unloading his groceries and looks at me but says nothing. It's the guy from outside yesterday.

After a short silence, he says, "I got ahead of myself yesterday."

"I guess we all do that from time to time," I say while begging for this interaction to end.

"It's part of the process," he says and takes his receipt and walks away without another word.

* * *

A woman with salt-and-pepper hair and deep-brown eyes is next in line. Before I can ask my typical questions, she grabs my hand. I pull back and try to shake away and remind her of social distancing. She leans in and says, "One day, you will look back on this time in life and smile. 2020 is as tragic and magnificent in direct proportion to any previous year recorded by humans. It just feels worse because we are wired in but less present in the moment. Do you know what I mean?"

"Ma'am, please let go of—"

"Maybe on that day, you will realize you were a hero to me and my family. Everyone is so fucking scared, and you're here. Underpaid and here. And I understand that you have to be here to pay the bills, but don't pretend the circumstance allows you to forgo proper acclaim. There are so many options in this world, but you chose to be here. I'm sure if you put in the effort, you could find some way to get out of the shit work. Maybe I'm being shortsighted. But does it really matter? You are here by choice and locked in by chance. I fucking appreciate it."

She pauses but then continues a moment later. "Most people will live their entire lives without anyone telling them that the work they do is essential. Almost everyone's job goes unnoticed for their entire lifetime. Do you foresee dental hygienists being referenced as heroes? I guess anything is possible, because we didn't see grocery-store employees as important before, but I can't imagine a scenario where marketing professionals are on the front lines of a virus. That says something profound about this moment in your life. You told me last week that you woke up after binging your whole life on someone else's dream."

"I told you a week ago?" I say, confused because I've never met her.

"You don't want what *they* want. In fact, I bet you feel a drift in your life. You spend your twenties getting fucked up on existential questions and alcohol, and now that you are in your thirties and you have the rutter in control, you need to find a direction. You are looking for something different. Well, you found it. Sometimes what you need and want are the same thing, and they are wrapped in coincidence. Then you end up in a grocery store during a pandemic. It's there you witness the raw nerve of humanity. It's overwhelming, but it's also simple on its face. This was always going to happen. It was inevitable. You might not know it now, but being a hero isn't about people running into buildings and carrying babies out. No, it can also be listening to people's problems and absorbing their pain with a measure of respect and being present with people who need you the most."

"Ma'am . . . I have never met you."

"You see thousands of people a day. I don't expect you to remember me."

"If we have, I don't remember. I'm sorry. But I need you to let go of my hand. This is not okay."

"That doesn't matter. You are still a hero."

"Ma'am . . . please let go of my hand."

"Did you hear what I said?"

A commotion begins behind her. "Hey, lady! Let go of the guy! We need to practice social distancing!"

The rest of the line joins in: "Social distance! Social distance!"

The woman grabbing my hand is undeterred. "Do you know that you are a hero?"

I pause for a moment and ask, "What makes me a hero?"

"Unforeseen sacrifice and determination."

The crowd continues to chant "Social distance!" behind her.

"Okay. Then I am a hero. I am certain."

"Why?" she asks.

"You just told me I am."

"You need to believe it. Not me."

"I believe I am a hero," I plead. My arm is sore from her grip, and her hot breath is in my face.

"Okay. Then why?"

"Because I have to put up with sanctimonious people like you."

She loosens her grip, looks me in the eyes, and says, "Exactly."

* * *

The next customer is stifled by tears. She blows her nose. Before I can say a word, she pleads with me to understand that her mother is in the hospital. And that I need to know this.

I tell her I understand.

"No, you don't!" she pleads.

"But I do. My grandmother is in the hospital also," I lie. I just want the conversation to be over with, but I want to fulfill my perceived duty as her guidance counselor.

"Really?"

"Yes. We are all in this together," I lie again. It's the only way to stop her torment—our torment.

She smiles and says, "Okay. Good."

At first, her response strikes me as cruel, but I quickly understand what she means. It's not her fault that she is stifled in her upper-middle-class world. I choose to work here, and I must live with my decision. She doesn't understand or care what it's like to have strangers dump their burdens on you over and over again. And you listen and console and empathize. It's my job. She may know what she is doing but not care either way. She just wants to know others are suffering too. We all suffer together.

Oddly enough, our interaction gives me hope and subdues the anxiety that's been creeping in all week. The fact that I understand her better than she does eliminates the plexiglass and six-figure income that stands between us. We are both human. Even though she thinks less of me. I know not everyone considers my job unimportant.

* * *

With my newfound sense of peace, it seems as if people flow through my line easily filled with quiet desperation and radical intent written on their faces. Small talk is at a minimum this morning. Only the beep, beep, beeping sound of items being sold fills the air. No commotion. No community. The soul has been lifted out of this place, and all that remains is the fear slowly crushing our emotional larynxes. With the silence comes, for once, a moment I'm not cursing the universe and loathing my day. Everyone is deep in their phones with tight jaws, hoping to read of a vaccine. They are looking for this answer from publications that thrive off of the consternation and hate they propagate every day. It's like telling the man robbing your house where you keep all the money but expecting him not to take it because you were honest. It doesn't make sense. And it's not a noble act. And it is one of the saddest parts of the longest songs in the world.

*　*　*

A woman with frail eyes steps into my line. She obeys the signage asking customers to practice social distancing and stays back from the customer ahead.

When she steps up to the glass, I ask how her day is going, to which I receive a negligible response.

That seems to be the norm this morning. Not every customer is interested in small talk or friendly greetings. Some just want to go through the line. No harm, no foul.

As I start placing the groceries in bags, I sense something is wrong when she puts her hand on her hip in disapproval and says, "I want them double bagged."

"I'm sorry, ma'am, we aren't supposed to double bag groceries right now since there is a paper shortage."

The loose skin under her arms begins to wobble. Tension is building all over her body. When people respond like this, you know that they've already prepared a magnificent complaint. They are lashing out against the world, and you are about to take the brunt of it. She is not pleased with my answer, and before I can back off and concede to her request, a hurricane of emotion arrives at my front door.

Her pupils shrink. The whites of her eyes double in size. She reaches past the plexiglass divider and rips the bagged groceries from the cashier stand and slams them into the cart. Her mask slips below her nose in her frantic scramble, and she tries to pull it back up.

Then she bends over the counter to take the items I had yet to put in the bag, looks me in the eye, and says, "It's not you." Then she throws the groceries at her basket, only to watch them spill onto the floor. She picks up one item and storms toward the exit.

I stare in shock at the surreal prime time newsclip transpiring before me. After storming past the other registers next to me, she turns around at the final cashier stand. And with the look of a rabid dog in her eyes, she yells something I can't hear, then licks her hand, throws it dramatically into the air, and smacks it down on the counter. She is out the door in an instant.

What a fantastic exit—a possible act of bioterrorism. I wish I could walk away with such enthusiasm and disdain for things outside my control. And, my god, the fire in her eyes. What an insatiable, primal, adversarial look she sent me. I put my hand down on the register and receive a shock from the surface. Everything is electric with a force I lack the words to describe. I'm breathing heavy. Little sunspots appear in my purview. I rest against the register. I think the next lady in line is talking to me, but I hear only muffled sounds.

That look in her eyes said it all. It transcribed all the pain and misery she must be going through. The troubled home. The disintegrating family. The god that left her behind. The chip in the windshield to her entire worldview and a dark cold winter around the corner.

Mike walks up to my register. "You doing alright, man?"

"Yeah, I'm fine. Did you see that?"

"Yeah, dude. Pretty fucking intense. I just talked to Rory about it, and he said she is already gone. But are you doing okay? Do you need a break?"

"Sure. I could use a breather."

"Okay. I'll send someone over."

My replacement arrives shortly. Now, I have fifteen minutes *all* to myself.

I peruse the aisles of my store for a moment. The shelves are near empty in almost every aisle. Customers are going out of their way to move five or six feet away from me like I'm a leper. I buy the last organic, fresh-pressed, locally sourced ginger lemonade left on the shelf. It's a godsend. Now I understand why people pay so much for groceries here. You pay for what you get with the ginger lemonade. Innocent cashiers will listen to your problems, wipe the conveyor belt after you put your filthy groceries into their life, and gracefully take your abuse when you flip out over the smallest thing.

By the time I sit down at the outdoor break area, I have only ten minutes left, and a heavy spring snow is falling like ashes from god's cigarette. Nothing is sticking to the ground. I watch a black Mercedes G-Wagen speed out of the parking lot. A woman is wearing a mask inside the jeep.

Every car that follows has a person wearing a mask inside. I realize that I'm still wearing my mask; I take it off. The choppy cold air hits my lungs. I don't smell the garlic from lunch anymore. I breathe in and out, then take a sip of my ginger lemonade, and for some reason I don't taste the deliciousness that I did just moments before.

One of the symptoms of COVID-19 is taste and smell going away. I can't smell anything. Is there anything to smell? What. The. Fuck.

Christian walks by and asks, "Aren't you cold, man? You don't even have a jacket."

I put my mask on quickly. "Ha. I didn't notice."

"What did you say?"

I pull down my mask and say, "Ha. I didn't notice."

"You didn't notice the cold? Are you sure you're okay?"

"I'm fine."

"What?" he asks.

I rip off the mask. "I'm fine, dude. Don't worry."

"Okay. I won't. Are you on break?"

"Yeah, for another . . . six minutes."

"Nice. Are you sure you aren't cold?"

"Yeah, dude. I don't think anything can be worse than going back in there."

"Ah, that's fair. Okay, I'll see you inside."

I have five minutes left now. Our break area sits in front of a set of windows facing the coffee bar and registers. Tina and Alejandro are talking to each other. I wonder why Tina hasn't been sent home yet. Was she the one who tested positive? Shouldn't she be quarantined? He is definitely upset. He's waving frantically and gesturing from side to side. Tina stands undeterred with a subdued look on her face. I feel slightly responsible for their quarrel. But my heart has grown cold on the matter. So much has happened since we talked. Behind them a hungry crowd waits, burning bright. Steam flows out from the exit door. But I'd rather wait until my time is up.

I contemplate quitting the job for a moment, but what would that say about my ability to withstand pain? I have always believed that we should be able to withstand pressure. We shouldn't fold so easily. With four minutes left now, my fingertips and toes are going numb.

A line still wraps around the building with Lindas and Daves and any other stereotype you'd like to include foaming at the mouth for their fancy American groceries. I'm sure some have tragic tales that I will hear about when I'm inside. The mirage of safety has faded away. But they won't talk about what we have *really* lost during the pandemic.

I wonder what would happen if Rory wasn't standing there with a loaded gun. Would they combine powers and run over poor Billy as he tries to count people going in? For some reason I doubt they would. Three minutes to go.

I take another sip of my ginger lemonade. Still nothing, and the snow continues to fall without accumulating on the ground.

Let's say I have COVID-19; I will probably survive, and I will get some extra paid time off. I take another sip of the lemonade. Now I can taste it. What the fuck? Is paranoia taking hold? This is high-end juice, for Christ's sake. I paid roughly a third of an hour's worth of work for this garbage.

Inside the store, Tina and Alejandro are yelling at each other. People are staring at them as they flail about. One of our managers walks up and motions for them to go upstairs, and all three disappear. The snow is piling up on my apron faster than it can melt. Two minutes left.

The people in line look underprepared as they huddle together for warmth and blend into the dollar-size flakes of spring snow. Their close proximity seems like an odd choice given the pandemic is still in full swing. Billy is in the neon-orange vest with white shoes. Those shoes will be ruined, but someone has to shag carts. The snow is falling fast and hard now, but only the ground is wet. Whiteout conditions. My beard is crusted up with ice, and the wind is pounding straight into my face. One minute left.

A man in a Maserati stops at the curb, rolls down the window, and snaps his fingers. "Hey, do you know where the local clinic is? We are going to get tested for COVID."

"Honestly, not sure. Maybe google it," I reply.

"Goddamnit, you people are useless," he says and rolls up the window and speeds off, almost hitting a customer on the way out.

Billy notices me from inside and runs outside. "Are you okay?" he asks.

"Okay?"

"Yeah, man. You are covered in snow. Let's get you inside. It's freezing out here."

I look at my watch. "It is about that time."

"Alright, man. Let's go," he responds.

"Where are we going to go?"

"Back into the heart of the matter," he says with a smile.

"I guess that's life on the grocery line."

About the Author

Adam lives in Denver, Colorado. He writes and blogs about all manner of things from life to beer to weird parts of his soul that he thinks are worth sharing. He doesn't love groceries but he does love food. This is his first book.

Acknowledgements

I could not have published this book without the contributions from these wonderful people. Thank You!

Aaron Schneider
Alex Posniewski
Amy Santos
Andrew Olmstead
Andrew Walker
Angie Welch
Anna Carlin
Anthony Mitchell
Ashley Archibeque
Bert Rothkugel
Billy Deal
Brandon Kelly

Chelsea Elwood
Chris Pruyne
Chuy and Arlene Delgado
Craig Kerkman
Dana Shepple
Darlene DiPasquale
David Garcia
Dustin Monroe
Ed Lovell
Elizabeth Schick
Esther Hwang
Gabriel Geiger
Holly B Tredway
J. Linn
Jenn Merck
Jeremy Holt
Jeremy Weinberg
Jimmy George
Josh Hamilton
Karen B. Hodges
Kathy Roth
Kelli Aimar
Kelli Bastien
Kelsey Hayden
Kenny Garcia
Kim Johnson
Kristin Ardourel
Kyle Benedict
Lauren Angotti

Acknowledgements

Lee Dananay
Leighton Peebles
Lidie Gorupic
Lindsay Rich
Lori Kaplan
Luke Hipsher
Mary Monroe
Matt Schick
Michael Walker
Milo Brannen
Minton Clark
Neil Ritenhouse
Nicholas Ryan Bennett
Nicole Donovan
Peter McCauley
Phyllis Wheeler
Rebecca Charles
Regyna Carbone
Ryan Mitchell
Sam Layle
Sara Randall
Stella Spalding
Taylor Wilson
Tiann Heit
Tyler Konecny
Ulysis Baltazar
Zachary McClain

Made in the USA
Monee, IL
16 October 2023

44723067R00108